Learning to Love Copy

Gigi Hodge

Contents

Dedication

To my husband, for everything you do and especially for your two-day trek through mountains, lakes, and jungles to get my new computer!

1

Seriously!

Michelle

"Oh, my frickin' God! Seriously?! No, no, no!"

"Ahh ... That doesn't sound like your usual first day of school excitement." I had called my best friend Aurelie on speaker as I pulled into the parking lot, so she could share my joy. Now my tragedy.

My heart sank as I surveyed the state of my Académie school yard, which had been immaculate before summer break. From a distance, the school resembled a quaint, old-fashioned red school house. However, on closer inspection, nothing was as it should be. With overgrown grass and broken windows, my once adorable school resembled an abandoned property. School was starting in less than a month, and Jeremy, my distant cousin, aka janitor/landscaper, had pulled a fast one on me and done nothing over the summer.

"Michelle Lynn LeBlanc! Use your words or I'm sending the sheriff over there! What's wrong?"

"What's wrong is that I'm going to kill cousin Jeremy. I'm going to kill him dead! It's a mess! Why, why, why did I let my mama convince me to hire my loser cousin as a groundskeeper? Guilt, Catholic guilt, that's what it was. She made me feel sorry for him because, as an ex-con, 'he's having trouble finding work'." I mimicked. "Perhaps, just maybe, that was more because he was a loser and not an ex-con." To ease the stress headache, I steepled my finger against my forehead and massaged in small circles.

"Deep breath, Shell. You will solve this problem. Hold on, I have to put you on speaker. I'm getting fresh croissants out of the oven."

"Okay." I took a deep breath. "I know I can solve this problem, but it will take time. I was so looking forward to hitting the ground running. My checklist for today included doing my start the school year paperwork. Now I have to deal with this."

"And you will deal with it. You just need to revise your checklist. Here you go, Ms. Clothilde. Watch that croissant, it is hot out of the oven."

In a state of panic, I whispered to Aurelie, "Take me off speaker phone!"

"You're off, now. Sorry! Safety first. I need both hands to work the oven."

I inhaled to find my zen. "Of course, safety first. It's just that Ms. Clothilde is on our board. They don't need to know about this. The silver lining in this fiasco was that I paid Jeremy in cash from my own funds, sparing the board from spending any money on my incompetent cousin. It seems those funds were siphoned off into the 'Jeremy Loser for Life' account. Ugh!"

"Aurelie, hand me that phone, young lady," Ms. Clothilde ordered in the background. Crap, I was toast.

"Michelle Lynn LeBlanc, tell me everything!" After a deep breath, I shared the sad story with Ms. Clothilde. Prevarication was futile; that woman always knew everything.

"What we need, and what I have been telling the board we have needed all along, is a permanent groundskeeper/ janitor. I'll talk to the board," she said. "Don't you fret."

"One more thing, Ms. Clothilde," I tilted my head and examined the, fingers crossed, not gang-related, graffiti on the interior courtyard wall. "We might need better security."

"I'll talk to that nice Richard, boy. He's doing security now. In the meantime, I have an idea. Why not hire a veteran? That way, the candidates will already have military background checks and they can help with security. I have someone in mind and will text you his contacts, but visit the HireVeterans.com website as well."

"It's gotta be better than 'Mama's Loser Employment Agency'. I'll work on that right now."

Ms. Clothilde cackled, and Aurelie came on the line.

"You got this Shell. Let me know if you need any help."

And so, instead of creating teacher schedules and starting on my welcome to school checklist, my day began with me posting a janitor/landscaper position on HireVeterans.com for immediate availability. Then I focused on cleaning my school until lunch. Fortunately, I wore my Rosie the Riveter inspired work clothes. While flexing my guns in the mirror, I told myself, "I can do it." Within the hour, my phone started dinging with job applicant notifications. I silenced my phone because I was in the zone.

By noon, I couldn't put off reviewing the job applicants any longer. Jumping in my old Volvo, I headed to Aurelie's cafe to review them on my phone while I ate lunch. Soleil Café was in Meauxville's *Le Carré,* or town square. Much smaller than the *Vieux Carré,* better known as the French Quarter in

New Orleans, our *carré* is a park surrounded by storefronts and St. Francis church. I found a shady parking spot in front of the church and took a short stroll past a few empty storefronts to get to Soleil cafe.

As I opened the door, the heavenly aroma of baked pastries and fresh-brewed coffee wafted towards me. With a skip and a smile, I greeted Aurelie with a peck on the cheek.

"Must have coffee and food!"

"Now, Rosie," she adjusted my bandana, "I need more details than that."

"I appreciate you recognizing my sartorial inspiration." With a flirty flutter of my lashes, I struck a pose to show off my fancy work ensemble. "My regular fall order, please."

"No pumpkin spice syrup, sorry. It's not fall yet for regular people. I'll add Cinnamon Dulce, your second favorite flavor … and to eat?"

"Everything bagel with garden vegetable cream cheese, please."

She glanced up from her iPad register. "I'm on it. For here or to go?"

My eyes wandered around the restful cafe, soaking in the calming atmosphere. "For here *s'il te plait*, I need a break from the cleaning and to select job applicants for interviews."

"I'll have that right out for you. So, not the first day of school you were expecting?" Aurelie asked as she fluttered behind the counter, getting my order together.

"Not even! Aside from shopping for Hello Kitty pencil cases with secret compartments, my first day back to school is my favorite day. As school director, I even get to go in early!" My favorite table was right next to the counter, and a plopped my purse on it.

Aurelie rolled her eyes. "You're such a nerd."

With a nonchalant shrug, I straightened my bandana. "Don't I know it!"

"I'm surprised you even took off a few weeks in the summer." Aurelie steamed my milk.

With a long, heavy sigh, I sat down. "Based on the state of my school, that might have been a mistake, but Nicole needed help. Plus, in the immortal words of Audrey Hepburn, 'Paris is always a good idea.' And bonus, my new niece's name is Ellie *Michelle* LeBlanc."

"And the baby daddy?" Aurelie asked as she pulled my bagel from the toaster.

"We don't mention Voldemort. He is persona non grata."

"Like sands in the hourglass..." Aurelie said, quoting her favorite soap opera, as she carried out my coffee and bagel.

I pulled out my phone. "Shh ... have to concentrate now. I'm selecting the person who will extricate me from this mess."

"Good luck with that!" Aurelie said and went back behind her counter to help another customer.

As I finished my coffee and bagel, I selected the top four applicants. Happily, Ms. Clothilde's referral was one of my top selections. Sweet. In my text to the board, I detailed my plan to conduct one candidate interview each day, incorporating yard work and cleaning tasks into the application process. By Friday, not only could I hire someone, but I could also assess the candidates' work while they cleaned up the campus. Plan approved, I waved goodbye to Aurelie and headed back to school.

Second star to the right and straight on 'til morning, I thought as I got back in my Volvo and drove to my Académie French Immersion Charter school. Once I arrived, I headed to my office fridge. Brilliant ideas deserved a reward, real Mexican Coca Cola in a green bottle ... yummy. Asking Siri to play a cheerful song, I did my happy dance as I drank my Coke. REM's *Shiny Happy People* started playing ... Perfect. Then I rolled up my sleeves and got back to work; our school year was back on track.

$$\text{\textcloseparen}\!\!\!\!\text{2}$$

The Test

Beau

"**S**tupid truck." I could *not* believe my luck. I finally landed a job interview when Big Betsy croaked out on me, so I had to hoof it. *Double time Marine if you don't want to miss the interview.* A glance at my watch reaffirmed my belief in the saying, 'It's better to wait than be waited on'. With twenty minutes to spare and two miles to walk in the July heat, I grabbed my bag, packed a clean shirt, and hoped nothing else went wrong. I needed time to clean up before my interview. *Murphy's law …* Just as my trek started, the skies opened up in a torrential downpour. The rain stopped halfway through my walk and a blazing sun emerged. Then my phone rang. Because what was one more thing?

I barked into my phone, without glancing at the caller ID. "What!?"

"Mal élévé! [*Bad manners*] Beau, is that how your mama taught you to answer the phone? I'm gonna have to speak with Denise about that." Ms. Clothilde had a way of making me squirm like an errant ten-year-old. Cue eye roll. Tangentially related to me by marriage. My Krewe (it's a Mardi Gras thing) called her the enlightened despot of Meauxville.

"Sorry Ms. Clothilde. I'm en route to my interview."

"You're welcome."

My eyes rolled again. "Thank you for the recommendation."

"Well, you needed something to do instead of forever wandering around your daddy's farm doing tasks you hate. That's no life."

"I don't hate it." In the shadow of St. Francis Church, I prayed lightning wouldn't strike me down for that lie.

"Don't love it either. Besides, when was the last time you were sociable and don't say your 'self-named' Krewe because those are your brothers. I mean, with people you haven't known your whole life. You're in a funk, moping around your big empty house. What you need more than a job is a good woman."

"Gotta hang up now, Ms. Clothilde. Thank you again for the job reference and for getting me out of my big, empty house."

"Now I could introduce you to one or all of my three lovely nieces —"

"Gotta go, I'm heading to the school. Bye." I took a calming breath, missing the Marines and our clarity of mission and purpose. A purpose that kept me from dwelling on... things. But today my mission and purpose was to get that job.

I arrived at the Académie French Immersion Charter School, an annoyed, muddy mess and sunburned, to boot. No worries, I headed into the boys' restroom right inside the gate to freshen up. As a Marine, I worried about security at the school as I slipped unnoticed onto campus. But the perfectionist in me needed time to make myself presentable before my interview. No one needed to witness my sweaty, muddy state.

With no soap or paper towels in the bathroom, 'freshening up' might have been an exaggeration. The bathrooms were a stinky mess. Think last day of festival porta potties. *Wow! This school needs help.* I held my breath and cleaned up as best I could.

As I left the restroom, I dried my hair with my old shirt, hoping it wouldn't leave a stench. I narrowly averted a collision with a petite, curvy female who was exiting the girls' restroom. She resembled a World War II pinup poster. Her enormous light brown eyes opened wide, and she took in a sharp inhalation.

With my hands held up in a non-threating a manner, I apologized, "Sorry, didn't mean to startle you."

"Guess both of us were working until interview time?" Her voice was Amy Winehouse's whiskey rough. As 'Back to Black' played in my head, Ms. Clothilde's suggestion hit home. If a prospective employer's voice distracted me during a job interview, maybe I should rethink dating.

With a shake of my head, I ordered myself, *Snap out of it, Marine!* "My, uh, my truck had an issue." Frowning, I took a breath to recenter myself. "I could have fixed it, but it came down to a choice of either fixing it and arriving late or hoofing it here double time. I chose the latter."

She beamed at me. "Punctual. Impressive. Since it is five degrees in the office and the air conditioner repair person won't respond to my calls, let's have the interview at one of our picnic tables." The picnic table she pointed to was in the shaded courtyard. My eyes scanned the campus. A charming red schoolhouse, modern buildings, and ancient live oaks surrounded that shaded courtyard. "Sounds good. I'll call my Marine buddy that does HVAC repair. He'll call you back to schedule, but priority in July goes to lived-in dwellings. It's a health and safety issue."

"Understood, thank you. As long as it's ready for my teachers by the end of the month. In the interim, my sweaters will get me through. Introductions first, I'm Dr. Michelle LeBlanc, school director. This is my French immersion school, Académie Immersion School. Originally, the old St. Francis Church, our school board preserved and renovated it into our school. Our board has the final say on your hire. However, they support the idea of hiring a veteran and you come highly recommended by one of the board members, Ms. Clothilde."

"She is my aunt by marriage, sort of. A kind of aunt-in-law? My sister is married to her nephew, so she has adopted me. Rather, she thinks she can tell me how to live my life." Oh God, now I was rambling. Stop Beau, now! "Ahem, just so you know."

"Yes, Ms. Clothilde likes to direct things." Dr. Leblanc was tactful. I snorted at that vast understatement. Dr. LeBlanc continued, "She informed the board she won't be voting on your hire if you're my selection. Do you have a resume?" I pulled a folder from my backpack and handed it to her. "Silver star, purple heart, this is all very impressive. Do you have any groundskeeping or janitorial experience?"

"Yes, but not for pay, so I wasn't sure if it should go on the resume. I've only ever been a Marine, and that job did not require a resume." She smiled at that. My palms got sweaty and tingled. *Was this how a heart attack felt?*

"Tell me about yourself then and why you think we should hire you." Her big brown eyes met mine as her pen poised to write on her clipboard.

"Beau Babineaux, former sergeant in the Marines from a family of Marines. It's the only paying job I've had. Started right out of high school at 17 and stayed in for 20 years. Before, during, and after that, I worked with my dad on his farm on the outskirts of Meauxville. Took care of the grounds, kept the barn and office clean, and even did security work when we were having issues with trespassing. Ms. Clothilde said you might need security. Like I said, I have experience, but never got paid for the work, unless you consider room and board payment."

Dr. LeBlanc was taking notes as she interviewed me, making check marks on a list. Her head lifted from the clipboard. "You don't want to work on your dad's property anymore?"

"Oh, I'll still be working there. That goes without saying. My house is on the family property. Thus, I'm obligated to work. What I want is a paying gig. Although I have a Marine pension, I'm too young to retire. Plus, the more time away, the less time to do the, shall we say, less interesting work. I'm not a farmer, ma'am. I need work to keep me busy, and I can do the job for you."

"Many people could do the job. Why should I hire you? *Vous venez de Meauxville. Parlez-vous français?*" [You come from Meauxville. Do you speak French?]

My response was in French, "Yes, since I was little, especially with my grandma. As a linguist in the Marines, I also speak Spanish, Arabic, Urdu, and Russian." She grinned and checked a box on her clipboard.

Then she tilted her head. "Since you were little? There weren't many families that still spoke French to their kids."

"From a family of Marines, ma'am. My pawpaw and dad knew how important languages were for national security. They taught us French at home and we learned Spanish and Russian at summer camp. The Marines taught me Arabic and Urdu."

"At the defense language institute," Dr. LeBlanc said, yearning on her face. "I always wanted to go there, in Monterrey. One day."

"What language do you want to learn?" I asked, distracted by the dark curls escaping from her bandana.

"Arabic, I'm part Lebanese and I promised my Jidew, that's pawpaw in Lebanese. Plus, Russian because it sounds good, 'Get moose and squirrel.'" Her Russian accent was deplorable. The corners of my mouth twitched, but I deadpanned.

"So I don't want to ruin my chances of getting the job, but I have to say that was the worst Russian accent I've ever heard."

As she laughed, more curls escaped her bandana and bounced free. They reminded me of the color of my favorite scotch, Lagavulin. *Focus Marine, get your head back in the game. This is an interview, not a date. Work not dating is your forte.*

"What can I say? It's based on years of watching 'Rocky and Bullwinkle'."

"No doubt, an excellent source for an accent, but I've seen the show and … uh … that is not what they sound like." This woman was a delight. I shook my head and frowned. These interactions were confusing and sidetracking me. This was a job interview. *Focus Marine.*

"Normal interview protocol suggests that you don't insult your prospective employer. You can double-check the Job interview 101 handbook, if you so choose." She tried to keep a straight face, but her lip twitched. I'd never been on a job interview, but I was pretty sure they weren't supposed to be fun. It'd been a long time since I'd had this much fun. *Head in the game, Marine.*

"Not a Marine rule or a Gibbs rule, so I don't know it."

"NCIS fan … nice. Points for that." She checked off something on her list. I tried to glance at her clipboard, but she blocked my view. "Nope, you gotta earn the checks."

I straightened. "How do I do that?"

"By answering my questions and doing a few tasks to help clean up the school." She pointed with her pen around the schoolyard. A very messy schoolyard.

"Tasks?"

"Just basic cleaning and yard work."

I nodded. "So basically anyone who interviews is helping you prepare the school … as part of the interview?"

Dr. LeBlanc shrugged. "How else will we know if your work is both up to our standards and fast enough? The job requires you to complete tasks while simultaneously cleaning up new messes the rascals will inevitably make."

"OK, let's get to the task. I'm much better at showing than telling." Dr. LeBlanc grew silent and then blinked her big, deep sherry eyes. Whiskey again … this woman made me think of smooth aged scotch.

My brow furrowed at that. "Did you get something in your eye?"

"What? No. Why do you ask?"

"You just did this weird blinking thing as if you were trying to get something out of your eye."

"I'm fine. Let me show you the room you'll be cleaning and the lawn you'll be mowing." With that, she gave me a tour and outlined the work and time requirements. "Okay, this classroom, that lawn, and in three hours you stop. After which I'll inspect your work and we'll have our business lunch. Oh … any food allergies?"

"Nope, but I have a very hearty appetite, so keep that in mind." She stilled and blinked again. "Something in your eye again?"

"Nope, see you in three hours. *Bonne chance.*" [Good luck]

All business. Except for that eye blinking thing. What was up with that?

The classroom mirrored the disorder of the school, with papers scattered and desks in disarray. After three hours mowing, cleaning, fixing and setting up the classroom, I waited on the adorable Dr. LeBlanc's verdict and the possibility of seeing her blink again.

3

Post-test

Michelle

While Sergeant Babineaux was working away, I seized on that time to complete tasks on my much-adored main administrative checklist. First, the mindless tasks were completed, such as preparing packets for teachers and parents. The copier was working … *Praise Jesus.*

As the copier printed, collated and stapled for me, I scanned my 'starting the-school-year' checklist and called Aurelie, who answered on the first ring. "Today is Ms. Clothilde's pick, Beau Babineaux, right? How is he?"

"Punctual." I scanned each item on the checklist. *He checks off all of my boxes. Bad Shell!*

"That's all you have for me? A big burly Marine. You should date him."

"What? No! No dating employees." Lowering the checklist, I wandered around my office, straightening as I went.

"So don't hire him," Aurelie said.

With a shake of my head, I said, "It's illegal to not hire someone just because they're hot."

"So, you think he's hot?"

Luckily, Aurelie could not see me blink. "I mean, I'm not in the market for dates. We just need someone to help with the school."

"Why not both?" she asked. "It's been a long, dry streak since you divorced Doug-ass."

As a cool, calm professional, I didn't rise to the bait. "Doug, was a mistake, no doubt, but I'm not calling to discuss my poor life choices. My purpose was to ask where you think I should order our lunch."

"What? You don't think he wants bagels and pastries for lunch?"

With a quick search of my phone apps, I clicked on the one for meal delivery. "For a six-foot something Marine, after three hours of hard labor?"

"Hah, you said hard."

"Oh my God, Aurelie, please." With two fingers, I massaged circles between my brows, a stress gathering location.

"Fine, try Pop's. They have hearty po-boys."

"Thank you. Now, how has your day been?" As she talked, I ordered from Pop's Po-boys. A six-inch for me and a 12-inch for Beau (blink). Mr. Babineaux of the hearty appetite (blink, blink). Plus a Mexican Coke, fries, and a sweet dough pie that they had on special added to each meal. Finished with the lunch order, I tuned back into Aurelie. I'm a terrible friend. What can I say?

"So, did you get to watch him do that hard labor?"

I laughed and glanced out the window. "The temptation was strong, but I resisted. I couldn't afford any more inappropriate 'I'll bet you are,' blinks."

"Oh, he made you blink, did he? That *is* promising!"

"Anyway, it wouldn't be fair. I didn't watch the other candidates as they worked, and I didn't want to make him nervous. Equal treatment for all candidates. Which means lunch, so thanks for the Pop's recommendation. Gotta go now and inspect his work."

"Far be it from me to get between you and your inspection of Beau Babineaux." Aurelie sniggered.

"Why are you my best friend? I need to get back to work. I'm finishing my 'starting-the-school-year' checklist, creating my pre-open house checklist, and finalizing the teachers' schedules." With that, I re-opened my Hello Kitty notebook.

"Yay! Checklists and flowcharts!" Aurelie quipped.

"You say that like those are bad things."

"Since you will probably run around doing school errands all day, I'll see you tomorrow for early morning joe. I want details." And with that, she hung up.

Details of what? At that moment, the timer rang. With my hiring checklist on my clipboard, I went to see Beau's work. He was on his knees, adjusting the last desk. The room was spotless. As I entered, he stood up, his sable hair fell into his bright blue eyes. The room appeared tiny compared to him; I felt tiny next to him. I blinked again. *Focus Shell.* Then I scanned the room. "Wow!"

"I forgot to ask the age of the students. The desks are bigger, so I adjusted them to a third-grade height. Will that do?"

I inspected the room. "Is this floor waxed?" He nodded. "How did you wax the floor? The buffer broke."

"By hand. Also, here are the parts needed to fix the buffer." He dropped them in my hand. "The riding lawn mower and drinking fountain both work now. The water from the fountain was *zirable.* [gross] That can't be healthy."

I raised my finger for silence and to process. Outside, he mowed the entire front and side lawns, not just his small section. Plus, the water from the fountain tasted fresh. Inside, the room was pristine, with perfectly aligned desks. I pulled out my phone and looked him in the eye as I called Ms. Clothilde, the school board president. "You were right, Ms. Clothide."

"Of course I was right. Right about what?"

I grinned. "Sergeant Babineaux, that's who. I won't take anyone else."

"Fabulous, I'll call a meeting to vote."

"No, I can't lose him. Text them and let them know that Sergeant Babineaux did the best job of all the candidates. In three hours, he not only completed the required tasks but also made over $4000 worth of repairs. With no job assurance! Plus, he speaks French. Tell them to hire Sergeant Babineaux or they can come down here on weekends and clean the school themselves."

Ms. Clothilde cackled again. "I love being right. Hold on."

"Uh huh ... I'll wait." Within five minutes, the board had texted their approval.

"I'll let him know," I told Ms. Clothilde, "and thank you."

"Your Mama raised you right. I'm happy to help." I hung up the phone to what resembled chortles and beamed at Sergeant Babineaux.

"You're hired! Let's see if lunch is here."

The delivery had arrived, and the driver had placed it inside the gate. Before I could pick it up, Mr. Babineaux scooped it up, sniffing the bags. "I've got that. It smells delicious! Where do you want it?"

I blinked again and stuttered, "Our picnic table, I mean, *the* picnic table. The one we used this morning when we talked." Sergeant Babineaux frowned and shook his head. Then I pointed, and he placed the bags on the table. I handed him his Po-boy to distract him and get my bearings again. It worked.

"Shrimp Po-boys," he said and took a deep inhale of the honey Sriracha sauce. "Hmm, both sweet and spicy. Thank you."

I pulled out my own Po-boy. "All part of the interview. These are Bang Bang Shrimp Po-boys, by the way."

"And fries and bottled Coca Cola. This is the best interview I've ever had!" He took a big bite of his Po-boy.

I grinned. "Does that include the three hours of labor?"

He nodded, but finished chewing before he responded. So good manners ... check. "Hey, you're paying and feeding me, and I like to work."

"Good thing, because I need you to start as soon as possible. I'll give you the paperwork, and you can bring it in tomorrow."

Before I could take another bite, he asked, "Can I just do it now and start right away? I'm kinda on a roll."

"Absolutely. Happy to have you on board. Any questions for me?"

He took a sip of his drink. "Vacation days?"

"I'll give you the calendar. When the school is out, you're off except in the summer I'll need you to come in once a week to keep this from happening." I gestured to encompass the messed up lawn, graffiti, and a broken window.

"What happened to the previous janitor? Groundskeeper? What did you call him?"

"*Jardinière* or *concierge*, whichever you prefer. Mr. Guillory wasn't full time. He worked for the public school board and did part time work for us. He retired in May. My mother convinced me to hire a distant cousin." I rubbed my forehead with my fingers.

Sergeant Babineaux shook his head. "Say no more. I once had one of those distant cousins helping take care of Babineaux land. The *couillon* [idiot] nearly burned down the barn. Useless!"

"Well, happily, he did not damage the school. In fact, he did nothing with the school. I was away, in Paris, for a few weeks helping one of my sisters, Nicole, while she took care of a newborn, and I couldn't check on the school. So, make sure you log overtime, but I'll be paying that out of my pocket. No sense making the school pay for my stupid decisions. If you meet my mama and she asks for anything … tell her no!"

He nodded. "Noted. Also, lucky you with a trip to Paris."

"You've been?"

"Yes, a few times, although I spent more time at SHAPE in Belgium." At my blank look, he clarified, "A Nato base, so military stuff. Traveled to Paris the last time with my friend Etienne. He has a relative buried in Normandy."

"Wow!"

We ate alternating between chatting about mutual acquaintances and enjoying the serenity of the afternoon. When we finished, Sergeant Babineaux took care of the trash and we headed to my office for paperwork and an afternoon coffee kick-start. I handed him the paperwork, showed him how to log his hours, and poured him a cup of coffee from the old coffeemaker.

"Thank you." He sipped and then grimaced. "This is *zirable*." [gross] At least he was honest.

"Getting a new coffee maker is on my checklist for today." Needing caffeine, I forced myself to drink the sludge. "Other questions?"

"What about trips to get parts? I wanted to head to Guidry's hardware to get these parts for the buffer." He showed me the bunch of gizmos in his hand. "Do I need to clock out?"

"Hmm, how about we estimate the time that will take you and add that to your timesheet. Note them here." I pointed on the timesheet.

"Works for me. I'm heading to Guidry's right away to get that buffer fixed before I tackle the other rooms. Also, I'm re-cleaning all the rooms. I want them all to my standard of cleanliness."

"Whatever you want to do. We have you on for full time. Just log your forty hours. If you need more hours to prepare for the teachers who will come in two weeks, let me know. I can authorize them easily enough."

"Will do, boss. I'm headed out. Do you need me to get anything for you?"

I scanned my office to determine what I needed. "Paper, printer ink, dry erase markers, pencils, pens, coffee, creamer, candy, extra notebooks, extra book bags, two coffeemakers, extra uniforms in all sizes, and underwear for kids."

His face scrunched in confusion. "Underwear? Schools supply underwear for kids? That's weird."

"For when they have accidents. We ask the parents to send spares, but if they don't, then we won't make a child run around without clean clothes. Oh, and we need snacks, canned goods, and other things to refresh our pantry."

"The school has a pantry?"

"No-questions-asked pantry. The kids, parents, and staff can go in at any time during school hours and get whatever they need. If you have extra plastic bags, bring them. We refill them as people use them in the pantry."

"That's ... nice."

I beamed at the compliment. "My teachers thought of it. They are brilliant. We want everyone to feel like it's a community. To avoid delaying you, I'll shop on my own."

"Time I can spare, plus you might need help carrying supplies."

"You may regret that decision, but yay! Road trip!" I put away my current checklist and filed Sergeant Babineaux paperwork. Then, on my way out the door, I grabbed my purse and the school credit card. "Also, that saves petty cash since I was going to have to pay you back for the parts, but now I can just charge them. Can we stop at Black Cafe on the way to Guidry's? I love their coffee and biscuits."

"Whatever you want, boss." We walked to the parking lot and Sergeant Babineaux stopped. "Crap, my truck died at a restaurant about two miles from here. Forgot about that. Can you give me a ride?"

"Serendipity." I jingled my keys and walked around my Volvo to unlock our doors. "Office Depot first, they offer an educator discount. See if there are any cleaning supplies you prefer there. Biodegradable only please. We will each take separate carts. We can do thirty minutes per store. Does that work for you?"

"Ah yes ... what's written on your car?"

I smiled at my old Volvo. "*Rugby players eat their dead.* I was hoping I had sanded enough off that it wasn't visible. This cool old car belonged to the intermural rugby team at Louisiana University. It's the only car I could afford after the divorce, but super sturdy and reliable." The edge of his mouth curled up and a hint of a smile flickered there. "C'mon. Get in. We will stop by that restaurant first to let them know you will be back for the truck later. Is it Country Kitchen Cuisine?"

"Yes."

"No problem. The Holliers have a grandchild at *L'Académie.* I'll text them to let them know we will get it later tonight. Ready to shop for supplies?" I pulled out my phone, texted, and nodded at the ding a few moments later.

"OK, all set. We'll spend thirty minutes at Office Depot, move on to the hardware store, and finish at Walmart."

4

Back to School Shopping

Beau

"**S**ounds good." Once I got in the car, her words registered. "Wait, did you say you could get all those supplies in thirty minutes? In a teacher's store? Not possible! My cousin Renee spends hours there. She works just to pay for teaching supplies."

Dr. LeBlanc backed out like a bat out of hell and then stopped. Her eyes met mine. "Does Renee speak French?"

"A bit of a non sequitur, but yes."

She engaged the clutch, shifted the Volvo into first gear, and sped off while I held on for dear life. "Enough to teach, say ... teach math or music in French?" She asked, focusing on the road.

"I'm not sure. Why?" I gripped the dashboard as she zoomed through town and made her way to Highway LA 31.

She threw me a notepad without taking her eyes off the road. "Write her contact information on this. I'm gonna headhunt her."

With a tightening tug on the lap belt, I asked, "You're gonna what?"

"Headhunt her, recruit her. If she speaks enough French to teach, I'll hire her this year. The music/art teacher backed out at the last minute, but we still have those funds. If her French needs work, I'll nominate her for a summer immersion teacher scholarship. We're always on the lookout for dedicated teachers, and especially French-speaking ones. If she is spending all her money on her classroom, she's dedicated."

I wrote Renee's number for her. "OK, I wrote it down, but I doubt she'll leave her school. She loves those kids."

"Now I really have to have her! I mean." Then she did that blinky thing again. *Odd.* After that, we sat in uncomfortable silence until we parked at Office Depot.

Once we arrived, Dr. LeBlanc unfolded a lengthy checklist from her notebook. "So, thirty minutes. We need to fill our carts and meet at the front to use the school credit card to pay for everything. Let me make sure I have my Educator discount card." Once we exited the Volvo, got our carts, and entered the store, it was game on. "OK, here are the rules ... thirty minutes or fewer. Get everything you need or want for cleaning. Betcha I can beat you back. On your marks, get set, go."

I shook my head and snorted as she ran off to shop. It was impossible for her to beat me. I asked a worker where I could find the janitorial supplies while she raced around the store to get her lengthy list of purchases. Setting my phone timer to twenty minutes, I figured had enough time to get what I needed and beat my adorable and apparently highly competitive new boss.

Dr. LeBlanc was waiting for me when I rushed to the front of the store after my timer rang. While my cart was full, full of cleaning supplies, she had not one but three carts of supplies. "I have it down to a science." She blushed. "Oh, and I win!"

"Coffee is on me." Then I helped her check out.

As we rolled the purchases to the car, she said, "My coffee order is pretty high maintenance. You sure you wanna offer that as my prize?"

I opened the Volvo's back hatch. "Yes, now especially. I want to see how complicated your order is."

"Excellent. Let's get this stuff packed up. Coffee, Guidry's and later Walmart for uniforms and pantry supplies." She looked at her watch, an old-fashioned delicate one like my Mawmaw Babineaux wore. A perfect addition to her pinup girl getup. "We're making excellent time."

As she zipped out of the parking lot, I asked, "Do you have a lot of work to finish back at school?"

Dr. LeBlanc grinned. "An endless amount, *comme d'habitude*." [as usual]

I held the dashboard as she zigzagged through traffic. "Sounds a lot like the military."

She glanced over as she executed a quick right-hand turn. "Except you're better funded."

"Very true, but not better paid." She chuckled at that.

We rolled into the Black Cafe drive through and the barista opened up the window to take our order. Dr. LeBlanc rolled down her window as well. "Afternoon. Do you have pumpkin spice yet?"

"Not until fall, ma'am," the barista said.

"No problem, I'll take a large mochaccino, add caramel, whip, and two shots of espresso, please. Oh, and an order of sweet potato biscuits." She turned to me. "Have you tried them?" I shook my head. "Make it two orders; I'm not a sharer." The barista smirked at that.

I added a small black coffee to the order and tried not to gawk at bill $25 bill for two orders of coffee and biscuits.

Dr. LeBlanc raised her eyebrows. "I warned you."

"That you did," I said as I handed over my credit card.

When the coffee arrived, she took her first sip of the brew and hummed her approval. "Yummy! We can snack on the biscuits once we get back. I don't want to get powdered sugar all over me … I mean, all over my car." She blinked again. Which made me want to peek into her brain and the box of sweet potato biscuits.

At Guidry's, I was in my element. I took over while Dr. LeBlanc inspected barbeque pits and knives that she was considering as gifts for her cousins.

"So whatcha got there, son?" The old timer, Mr. Guidry, said when I moved up to the counter.

I showed him the broken pieces. "Parts to a floor buffer for the Académie French Immersion School."

Mr. Guidry scratched his chin. "Don't think we got those parts. Might need to machine them."

"How long? School starts at the beginning of August and I gotta a lot of floors to polish."

"A week?"

I nodded. "That works. I can find something else to do for a week. Should I pick them up here?"

"L'Académie, huh? My grandchild lives near that school. She starts school next year. How about I drop the parts off over there? I wanna check out the school."

"That's perfect." Dr. LeBlanc interjected over my shoulder. How she heard Mr. Guidry from across the store was a mystery. "If you have an address, I can also send you a brochure. We're always looking for promising students. I'm Dr. Michelle LeBlanc, Mr. Guidry. Ellie Mae and Bruce LeBlanc are my parents."

"Ellie Mae, I remember her. Crackerjack, from up north, but from good people."

"Yes sir, from the Cajun borderland of Alexandria, Louisiana." She grinned. "And this here is Sergeant Babineaux, our new school concierge."

"Concierge, is that just a fancy name for a janitor?"

"Not at all. Sergeant Babineaux runs all the physical parts of the school and even helps with security. I don't know how I have gotten along without him. If you ever need to hire somebody, get in touch with HireVeterans.com. He is a godsend, I tell you. In less than three hours, he mowed our lawns, fixed our riding mower and drinking fountain, diagnosed the issue with our buffer, and shopped for school supplies. Three hours, Mr. Guidry!"

"Wanna job?" Mr. Guidry asked me.

"Oh, no you don't. He's mine!" I smiled smugly at that, Mr. Guidry smirked at me, and Dr. LeBlanc just blinked.

"He might just be. But a hard worker can always find work. Come see me if she don't treat you right." He winked at me.

I shook his hand. "Yes sir. We'll call that Plan B. In the interim, see you next week."

"And I will happily show you around our school, even though you tried to poach my concierge." Mr. Guidry cackled and put the parts in an envelope. As we walked out of there, she said, "Can you believe the nerve of that man? I just hired you."

I held the car door open for her. "Well, if you would stop telling everyone what I did this morning, that might keep the recruiters at bay. Walmart next?"

"I know, but it's so impressive. Apparently, I have to be more circumspect." She checked off more items on her list as I got in. "Pantry and pants next on the docket."

Dr. LeBlanc called ahead to one of her parent, Ms. Susan, who worked at Walmart. "They're giving me mystery cans for ten cents each and their old bread for free. Since our school uniform can be any uniform bottoms with any uniform shirt, we can get all the tag-less returns for five dollars each. I use petty cash for the food and clothes because certain board members will grouse if they think we used school funds for that."

"So what is petty cash supposed to be for?" I asked.

"Snacks for training, open houses, and celebrations. The teachers and some of our parents take care of that so we can use the funds on uniforms and the pantry."

"I'm starting to really like your school," I said as she parked in the Walmart parking lot.

"Our school," Dr. LeBlanc said as she got out, closed the door, and walked into the store. Inside, she hugged one of the Walmart workers, Ms. Susan, I assumed. Then she shook hands with the manager. They spoke for a moment. After that, she covered her eyes with her hands and tears cascaded down her cheeks. I double timed it over there to see what happened.

"Really? There are no words to thank you." She turned and looked at me. "Sergeant Babineaux, Mr. Jones is giving us the canned goods and uniforms for free! They think our pantry idea is a good fit as a community project for their store and they want to come by and see how ours runs. We, ahem, we can't thank you enough! It has been a tough year for some of our students."

Mr. Jones grinned. "Just see if you can get your parents to buy their supplies here. Either way, we want to do this, and you have made our store look good by bringing this program to corporate."

Dr. LeBlanc beamed at Ms. Susan. "Susan, for Open House, we always give gift cards. We'll get them all here. Here are the funds we were going to use on our pantry and uniforms. Can you get me gift cards in twenty-five dollar increments?"

Mr. Jones grinned. "Add four more cards from us and charge it to management, Susan."

"I will not embarrass you by hugging you, but understand that in my mind you're getting hugged like crazy."

Mr. Jones laughed. "Good to know. Let us know if you have any other innovative projects. We want to be the first to help."

"Absolutely! While we wait on the cards, I need to look for a new coffee machine for my office and the lounge. Gotta keep those teachers caffeinated! Thank you again. You've been a blessing on our school."

"Happy to help." Mr. Jones shook Dr. LeBlanc's and my hands.

"You see how wonderful people can be?" she said as she led me through the store.

When we finished, she had two fancy coffee makers, several coffee pods, and a mini-fridge. As she checked out, Susan handed her the gift cards and directed me over to two large carts full of canned goods and uniforms. Tears were welling in Dr. LeBlanc's eyes as she admired the over-flowing shopping carts. Then she plunked down what was clearly *not* the school credit card and swiped it to pay for the coffee, coffeemakers, and fridge. *Teachers.* I shook my head.

5

Man Cave Weekend

Still Beau

"And then she just paid for it all with her own credit card. Who does that?" I was hanging with my long-time friends from elementary school at my house. Once a critical mass of mischief, my friends and I had transformed into law-abiding, contributing citizens.

"Teachers?" Marc responded.

Marc Richard was my best bud. He was now serving in the Air Force Reserve. Formerly a lieutenant in the Air Force, Marc had dedicated himself to his career. But everything changed when he became a single dad to sweet Sofia. Wanting to be there for his family, he transitioned to the reserves. Mawmaw Richard, Marc's grandmother, was watching Sofia, so Marc could hang out. Marc, with his steel-rimmed glasses and pocket protector, gave the impression of an engineer, not an airman. The Air Force goes for those brainy types. He uses those brains to run a state-of-the-art security company. He is all about providing for Sofia.

"You have teachers in your family. This is not news to you. Weren't you complaining the other day when we moved your cousin Renee, from the apartment she couldn't afford, to the shack over her aunt's dress shop? You said something to the tune of, 'well, if you wouldn't spend all your money on your students, you might could afford a nicer place'."

I grimaced. "Did I say that?"

"Had to hold Renee back from belting you," Armand said.

Armand Leger was an Army Ranger who rarely had leave time. He hadn't been able to hang with us in over a year, since we set Renee up in her new digs. A troubled straight-shooter, he was our chick bait when we went out. His looks made the girls swoon. He looked normal to me. Dark hair, dark eyes, pale skin. Maybe they thought he resembled a vampire? According to my mama, he was French Creole, hinting at a lineage which traced back to French landowners. Anyway, he had his uses.

"She's a protector." We rolled our eyes at Etienne.

Etienne had been in the Navy. He used to hang out with Theo, my older brother, before Theo had been killed in action in Afghanistan. Marc, Armand, and I had sort of inherited him. He was a cousin to my brother-in-law Alex, my sister Gelly's husband. They kinda looked similar. My sister would go on and on about her caramel colored cowboy. Which is just weird if you ask me, but yeah ... he and Alex likewise called themselves Creole. In Louisiana, it's complicated. Anyhow, Etienne, a deputy with sheriff's office, was trying to become a profiler with the FBI. He was working on his psychology degree and annoying his friends by constantly diagnosing their behavior.

"Is that a real psychological term?" I asked.

"It is on the Myers-Briggs personality test, an ISFJ personality, to be exact. They are warm, caring, and they protect anyone that they think is in their group, anyone they care about."

Considering Dr. LeBlanc's 'our school' statement, I wondered if I now belonged to her tribe. I hoped so.

"Maybe she makes a lot more than her teachers and feels guilty. A lot of those charter school CEOs make a ton of money.

Renee was complaining to me the other day that they were stealing all the public school money," Armand said.

"How?" I asked, wondering if my 'good girl' image of Dr. LeBlanc, Michelle, was mistaken.

"How am I supposed to know that? I was just trying to get Renee to finish her drink so I could walk her home before Cowboys got rowdy."

"You were drinking with my cousin in a bar?" I narrowed my eyes and glared at Armand.

"No, jeez, I went there with some buddies and when I arrived, she was waving goodbye to some friends. 'Friends,'" Armand did air quotes, "who left her there tipsy, by ... her...self. You know what a happy drunk she is. She thinks everyone is her friend ... at a *dive* bar like Cowboys!" Just the thought of it made Armand seethe.

"Yeah, Renee is, without a doubt, a 'Caregiver'," Etienne said.

"Well, she is a teacher." Armand shrugged.

"No, in the Myers-Briggs classification, she is ESFJ, 'The Caregiver'. They are soft-hearted and believe the best about people. Those people need protection."

"True Dat. Thanks Armand. I'll call my cousin Jeb and let him know he needs to be more vigilant."

"Already done, but you can remind him, and give Eric and Kevin a sitrep as well. All her brothers need to know." Armand and I both knew the repercussions for informing her brothers. Snitches get stitches, but tough shit. Maybe we were 'protectors' too.

"Hey, Etienne," I asked, "what are protectors who aren't nice and caring and don't believe the best about others? Is there a type for that?"

"Maybe the Director or the Commander. I need a project for my senior honors thesis. I could do all of your Myers-Briggs personalities and then compare them to your life trajectories."

"Life trajectories, nerd." Mark snorted.

"Well, the FBI doesn't take dunces. Besides, if by nerd you mean smarter than you, then yes, yes, I am." Marc tackled Etienne to the ground.

"A Navy versus Air Force SmackDown!" Armand raised his beer to them.

"Battle of the wimps!" I shouted. Etienne and Marc stopped wrestling long enough so they could both give me the finger.

"Good times!" I said to nobody in particular and took another sip of my Lagavulin. The color reminded me of Michelle's curls. Not Michelle, Dr. LeBlanc ... my boss.

After Marc and Etienne finished their brawl, both claiming victory for themselves and their military branch, they grabbed another brew and got comfortable by the fire pit.

"Can you ask Renee about the Académie French Immersion Charter school?" I asked Armand.

"Sure, she goes to Cowboys every Friday with the other school teachers. I'll get there before they begin drinking or, as they call it, 'Choir Practice'." Armand air-quoted.

"Choir Practice!" Marc snorted. "Is that what they call it nowadays?"

"Renee said that is what they announce at school on Fridays. 'Choir practice at the usual place'. Which is code for drinking at Cowboys." Armand shook his head.

"You sure do talk to Renee a lot." I raised an eyebrow.

"No, I go to Cowboys when I have free time, because I'm a man and that is where to go to find horny chicks."

I cocked my head to the side. "Armand, did you just call my cousin a horny chick?"

"What!? God, no! Renee hangs out there because she's a poor teacher and wants someplace to go after school that won't break her budget if she gets a few drinks. They have cheap beer. Plus, she lives near there, so she says she can walk home."

Silence reigned around the fire pit after that statement.

"No one is going to let her walk home by herself and drunk to boot. I paid the bartenders and waiters to call me or her brothers if they see her leave alone or with a guy."

"You are *so* going to get in trouble. Put me on the list to call as well. In case you are both busy or not responding," I said.

"Me too!" Marc raised his hand. "I can stash Sofia in her car seat and go get her."

"Me three!" Etienne added. "Plus, Cowboys is in the sheriff's district. I can get any of my buddies to pick her up and put the fear of God into anyone trying anything with her."

"Renee's going to love that!" Armand smiled.

We went back to drinking, but I wondered if my first impressions of the lovely Dr. LeBlanc were incorrect.

After sipping our libations and watching the fire, Armand interrupted.

"Beau, can I crash here for the rest of my leave?"

"Sure, I have four empty rooms and an office. Take your pick."

"Why can't you stay at your mom's?" Marc asked.

"She has frequent 'guests'," Armand air quoted again.

"TMI! Do not tell me about your mom's love life." Marc put his hands over his ears.

"Seriously, and I don't want to see it. Plus, I think it will be a relief for her. We have had some very uncomfortable morning coffees with the 'friends' doing the walk of shame back home. She always brings them in her car and then she won't drive them home. Very uncomfortable."

"You're welcome to stay at my home as long as you want. There's plenty of room. Take your pick of rooms. As long as you promise to never again reveal anything concerning your mom's love life to me, ever, again."

"Deal. I have my stuff in my truck."

"We can help you bring it in," Etienne stood.

"Nah! I just have my duffle. I don't really have much." With that, Armand headed to his truck to get his belongings.

While Armand moved his things in the house, Marc turned to me and asked, "Speaking of which, why did we help you build a house with four rooms?"

"Because, back in the day, I believed I would have a big family that would love to live on a farm." That dream was dead.

"But," Etienne said, "I thought you hated farm work. Isn't that why you're working at that Académie school?"

"Yes, but what I learned from my father is that if you have kids, you can just supervise and you don't need to do the hard work. So, I wanted to make sure I had plenty of kids, but Marine life and family life or even couple life don't mix."

"Well, you aren't in the Marines anymore, plus, now you've got an entire school full of kids to take care of." Marc laughed.

"It's doubtful Dr. LeBlanc will let me use them for farm labor."

"In my experience, it is all in how you frame things," Etienne said. "If you make it an educational experience, you might could get them to harvest all the garden veggies, pick up the eggs, and clean the horse stalls."

I raised an eyebrow. "I might need some help with the wording to sell her on that idea."

Armand made his way back and poured himself a couple fingers of Lagavulin. "Thanks man. What did I miss?"

"Beau is trying to think of how to convince his boss to use the students as farm labor for an 'educational experience'." Etienne filled him in.

"Renee says administrators never listen to teachers. I doubt she would listen to a janitor."

"Hey!" I flicked ice cold water from the ice chest at Armand. "I'm not a janitor, I'm a *concierge*."

"Whatever man." Armand said, while we continued watching the fire and listening to crickets chirping.

6

Bunny Day

Michelle

Choosing a 1940s esthetic once more this morning, I wore overalls and styled my curly mahogany hair in double rolls with side braids similar to Heddy Lamar in *Tortilla Flat*. As the pièce de résistance, I threw on my pink Converse high tops, which technically were from the same era, but for girls, they're an anachronism.

Time for coffee, fancy coffee. I headed down the garage steps. My mama, the early bird, was in the front yard gardening.

"Where you headed, sweetie?" Ellie Mae LeBlanc is a 'butter would not melt' on her tongue, Southern Louisiana Belle. There's a rumor that Rodrigue's famous *Jolie Blonde* painting was inspired either by her or her mama, maybe even both. Despite living together for nearly thirty years, I'd never witnessed her without hair styled and makeup done.

"Soleil and then the wonderful Académie French Immersion School," I said, kissing her cheek.

"It's wonderful you love your job and look how adorable!" She made me spin around to check out my ensemble.

"Thanks. I'm off to school to clean up the mess that my hiring Jeremy left behind." I gave her a fake glare.

"Stop that." She tugged on a braid. "Someone had to give him a chance. He's family."

Groaning, I said, "Distant family."

"But family nonetheless. Don't fret, it's nothing you can't clean up. Plus, you did your good deed for the year. Before you head out, go tell your daddy, bye." She shooed me away.

With a smile, I skipped up the porch steps and into my father's arms. He was standing on our big front porch with coffee in hand.

"You want a cup?" He lifted his coffee cup, which smelled divine, but I resisted.

"No, I'm holding out for the good stuff at Soleil."

"Tell Aurelie we said hi," Mama yelled up from the garden.

"Of course."

"Off to school?" He kept his arm around my shoulders as he talked. Kinda a half-hug to let me know he wasn't ready for me to walk off yet. While mama gives off beauty queen vibes, daddy was Mr. Rogers personified, even down to the cardigan. Although his sweater was lighter, a nod to the Louisiana heat. Wool sweaters in summer won't do.

"Yes!" I laid my head on his shoulder. Comforted by the smell of his coffee breath and Old Spice. Daddy kissed my cheek, smiled, and handed me an envelope.

"What's this?" It felt sturdier than a letter.

"A new school year present to my favorite principal."

"School director," I corrected.

"What's the difference?"

With a grin, I opened the envelope. "No difference, it just sounds fancier. Gift card for Soleil café, score!"

"That is for you! Don't go buying coffee for your faculty with that."

"Of course," I said in my most innocent voice, already thinking of back to school treats for my faculty.

With one last hug, Daddy said, "Now, get out of here and have fun."

"Always do," I said and hopped in my beat up old Volvo to head to Soleil for a fancy coffee.

I arrived bright, early, and caffeinated to school, hoping to check a few tasks off my lists in the early morning calm. As I was getting started, at the crack of dawn, Sergeant Babineaux drove up in his beat up old pickup truck. Clearly trying to make a good impression with his punctuality.

My mind strayed as I watched him. His sable curls kept falling into his eyes as he took what appeared to be tools from his truck. He must have gotten frustrated with his hair, because he finally pulled the curls back and secured them with a baseball cap. He needed a haircut. I blinked, imagining running fingers through that hair. *Bad Shell*!

Smiling at his expression, I saw the moment Sergeant Babineau realized he didn't have any keys to the building. His big blue eyes widened, and he looked around. I pulled away from the window, cuz I'm not a creeper. Then I waited for him to notice the light in the office. Five minutes later, a knock sounded on my exterior office door.

"Who is it?"

"It's me, Beau, Dr. LeBlanc."

"Already?"

"My sentiments exactly. I guess we are both early risers. Can I come in?" Sergeant Babineaux nodded his head in approval when I looked through the window before opening the door.

"C'mon in, Sergeant Babineaux." I gestured as I opened the door.

"Nice job checking before opening the door, Dr. LeBlanc, but you need a door with a peephole." He examined the door and said, "One that's lower than the standard peephole."

I cocked my head and squinted. "Are you calling me short?"

"Uh ... they are just safer if you don't need to climb on a chair to see through them."

I put my hands on my hips. "You are calling me short!"

"No, I mean."

I chuckled. "No, really, I'm just messing with you. I can be difficult in the mornings."

"Really? Good to know, Dr. LeBlanc." Sergeant Babineaux's eyes met mine.

Don't blink, don't blink, don't blink. Then I blinked. I'm somewhat certain he noticed. Again, he didn't smile, instead he cocked his head and frowned, as if trying to figure out a puzzle. Time to change the subject. "Please, call me Michelle. It is going to be strange if you're always 'Ma'aming' or 'Doctoring' me."

"Michelle." He repeated *sotto voce*. "Please call me Beau."

"Okay, Beau, what are your plans for today?"

"Since we are waiting on the floor buffer parts, how about I get the lawn edging and the outside of the school spiffed up?"

"Perfect! Don't want the parents to think the school looks abandoned." Beau scanned my office. To him, it no doubt resembled the aftermath of a hurricane, with debris scattered everywhere. He couldn't recognize the method to my madness.

"Unless you need help in here ... with all this." He indicated my chaos by waving his hands around.

"That depends. Do you have room at your parent's farm for six new French teachers? I'm working on welcome packets and making sure they have a host family." The sight of my long checklist for the day sent me into panic, prompting me to straighten the files and acci-purposely cover it.

"A host family?"

"You know, a community member who lodges them, speaks a little French, and can help them find a car, an apartment, and whatever else they need."

"Hmm." Beau reflected and then got out his phone. "My grandma, Mawmaw Babineaux, might could help. Let me give her a ring. Then you can explain to her what you need ... in French." Beau winked at me, dialed, and then spoke to his mawmaw. "*Mawmaw, parle avec Dr. LeBlanc s'il te plait elle a des idées.*" [Grandma speak with Dr. LeBlanc please, she has ideas] He handed the phone to me.

"Call me Michelle. You're making me feel old," I whispered as I took the phone.

While I was trying to convince Mrs. Babineaux to use her contacts to find host families; Beau got to work. At noon, I sent him a text.

"Lunch is on me! Your grandma got me five host families!"

As Beau walked in, he took off his hat and his sable curls escaped. He was big, buff, and sweaty. I blinked, imagining grasping his curls while pressing against his giant sweaty body, but just for a second. First and foremost, I'm a professional. *Maybe I should try dating again.* Then I realized my eyes had been closed through that entire train of thought. *Merde!* [Shit!] When I opened my eyes, he was staring at me with furrowed eyebrows. No doubt debating if I had a mental condition. Well, that works.

"Something wrong?" I asked.

"Uh, no, I, uh, was just waiting for you to open your eyes. I finished sealing the new window and mowing."

"You are the best, best hire! Ever! Mrs. Babineaux went above and beyond by not only finding me host families but also offering to take part in our Culture Fridays. She'll be showing the kids how to make a roux from scratch." Exhilarated, I bounced around the office while I cleared clutter off the chairs so we could sit. "The food is by my desk. Can you clear a place off the table while I freshen up? Throw nothing away! Just put it on the floor, somewhere."

Staring in the faculty bathroom mirror, my cheeks were red from exertion. My carefully styled double rolls were now a tad crazy, so I smoothed out the rolls, pulled out a few face framing curls and redid my two braids. *Heddy Lamar would be proud,* I thought. A dab of lip gloss, the alphabet song as I washed my hands, and I was ready.

We settled at the edge of the meeting table to eat. Beau had stacked my papers in neat piles on the other end of the table. As I pulled the Social restaurant bags toward me and opened it, Beau peered over my shoulder.

"Fried green tomatoes. Mmm! I hope you got two orders. Those are my favorite."

I smiled at his eagerness. "Valuable information." I pulled out a second identical box.

"Excellent! What else is in that magical bag?" For a taciturn guy, he was animated when it came to food.

"For you, an order of boudin flatbread and a Reuben sandwich, and for me, a beet salad and shrimp and grits." After I distributed our meals, we dug in.

"You eat very well for an educator."

That odd statement stopped me in my tracks. I gave him my best, *explain yourself* look. When that did not work, I used my words. "What do you mean?"

"Umm...I just mean, umm ... my cousin Renee. She teaches and umm ... can't afford anything but drink specials on Friday at Cowboys."

"Are you saying I get paid too much?" I raised my eyebrow. The same move I used to terrorize errant eleven-year-olds.

"No, I ..." Beau did not know how to respond. "No. I didn't mean that. I, uh, meant thank you for the food, and I will shut up now."

After a few moments of stilted silence, I cleared the air. "I make more than most public school principals, but that's because we don't have a full-time vice-principal, a curriculum coordinator, or a disciplinarian. I fulfill all those roles. We only have a part-time assistant director, in case of emergency and for overflow work. However, we are not like those corporate charters that claim to be nonprofits, but whose corporate branches make money on exorbitant school construction and leasing fees. We spend our funds on experiences for the students, books, supplies, and in house educational services."

"Sorry. My friend Armand was talking to Renee."

"Renee, your cousin, the dedicated teacher who speaks a little French, Renee?"

"That's the one. Armand said she was bitching about charter schools taking money from public schools." I grabbed my Hello Kitty notebook and jotted down notes.

"What are you writing?"

"Just making recruitment notes to be transparent about where we spend our funds when I speak with her."

Beau shook his head. "Are we okay?"

"Absolutely. You weren't trying to be insulting. You were just ill-informed, and I informed you how our school works. It's what educators do." With a wink, I continued eating, and changed the subject. "So, how is the exterior work progressing?"

Beau let out a big breath. "Like I said, I mowed the entire lawn and painted over the graffiti, but I took a picture of it first."

"Why?"

"In case it denotes some kind of gang. It's possible it's just a bored punk artist looking for a medium, but if it is a territorial sign, we might have more work to do in terms of security. I sent it to my buddy Etienne. He works for the Sheriff."

I stopped eating. "Should I be worried?"

"Naw ... chances are it is nothing. That was just a precautionary measure. So, the outside looks good. After lunch, I'm cleaning the bathrooms, since the tile floors don't need to be buffed."

"Wow! We might run out of work for you." I took a big bite of my salad.

"I doubt it. If you do, you can have the teachers create a diagram of how they want their rooms set up. Renee always forces me to set up her room. I've done rows, pairs, trios, small groups, and even a large broken U."

Wiping my mouth with a napkin, I asked, "Broken U?"

"It has kids in a U shape around the perimeter of the room but with a pass-through so Renee can get to all the students without delay." He motioned for my notebook and then drew me a diagram of the broken U. He tried to hand the notebook back.

"Smart. Can you create more diagrams of desk configurations? I'll send out a survey for the teachers to choose how they want you to set up their rooms?"

He shrugged and sketched out a bunch of options. Before he handed me back my notepad, he flipped over the cover and smirked.

Lifting my shoulders, I shrugged. "What? I like Hello Kitty."

"My sister, Gelly, and Renee had everything Hello Kitty growing up."

"Ah yes, Renee. Anything else you do for Renee?"

"Occasionally, I help her with school supplies. The parents bring supplies in and Renee organizes a table in the back of the classroom. On the table is a picture of each item showing its designated spot and a supply checklist for each child."

"Yay! Checklists! I'll print our supply checklists for each student and grade level. Can you make sure there is a table at the back of each room? Our parent volunteers can move the supplies to each teacher's storage closet. These are great ideas or, as we say, you have a *bunny day*." I took a big bite of my shrimp and grits.

"A *bunny day*?"

Finishing my bite, I beamed. "It is a joke. 'Good idea' in French. Get it?"

"*Bonne idée* sounds just like Bunny Day. Funny." He said 'funny', but he didn't smile.

With a slide, I gave my notebook back to him. "Anything else?"

"Are you always this open to suggestions?"

"I like bunny days and you are brimming full of them. What else?" Beau's mouth twitched. It happened in the blink of an eye. Nearly missed it. At this point, he must have been doubting my sanity.

"Well, I know Renee's major frustrations with teaching include the lack of breaks, hurried lunches, and the inability to use the bathroom. Which is weird because I thought US labor laws required all three of those things."

"Well, those are problems with many public schools, but our school has resolved many of them. Lunch is not a problem. The PTA and teacher aides watch the kids from lunch to after-lunch recess. In addition, because we are immersion, each teacher gets one hour of planning which, if they plan at home, they can use as a break. For bathroom breaks, I'll add a code for calling the office. Something amusing that the kids will understand later. *Les pissenlits ont bien marché.* That'll work."

"The dandelions worked?"

"In French dandelions are called 'pee in your bed', because they're a diuretic. So saying the dandelions worked means they have to use the restroom. Adding it to the faculty handbook now. Teachers can call the office, and we'll send someone to watch their class for a few minutes. Elementary kids love any jokes pertaining to bodily functions."

"I'm parrain [godfather] to a five-year-old, so I have read my share of 'Everybody poops', more than my share." Beau finished his meal and threw away his compostable containers.

"The school library has five copies of that book." I chuckled as I pulled out his containers and put them in our compost bin outside the meeting room door.

Beau followed me outside. "And on that note, I am going to clean the restrooms. There are dandelions growing in the field next door. Do you want me to dig up some of them and plant them outside of the outdoor bathrooms in the courtyard?"

"Yes! So fun! You are brilliant! This is going to be a fabulous year!"

7

Meet the Heberts

Beau

The next two weeks passed smoothly. I prepared everything for the teachers, including setting up their desks according to their selected designs. The school was spotless and everything was working well. Most of the teachers were already setting up their rooms. I was there to help move materials from their cars. They brought so much from home, benches, bookshelves, rocking chairs, and other sundry items. If this is what teachers with a $1000 a year budget needed to bring to the classroom, I needed to give Renee more gift cards. Plus, I called Armand to help her in her room since I had my hands full with Académie Immersion School.

My daily tasks included moving materials, lifting boxes, reconfiguring workspaces, and even providing impromptu car maintenance for two dilapidated cars. Michelle was a whirling dervish. She helped the teachers set up their room, got their books into the students' desks, and planned out their first day. She liked them to plan at least the first day to the hour. So they felt totally prepared. In each classroom, I installed the supply tables with laminated supply checklists. This impressed the teachers. Michelle underlined that the tables and supply sheets were my 'bunny day' as was the 'pissenlit' code that she added to the faculty book. They genuinely appreciated that. Besides the help Michelle provided the teachers, she was giving school tours, and meeting with parents and board members. Clearly, she needed more than twenty-four hours in a day. Lost in thought as I watched Michelle, I did not notice the young girl that stepped into my path.

"*Pardon Monsieur Babineaux.*" [Excuse me, Mr. Babineaux] She edged around me.

"*Bonjour*, how did you know my name?" She looked to be around ten or eleven with big brown eyes, wavy brown hair, and a my-baby-sister-cut-my-hair-in-my-sleep haircut.

"Madame Michelle was talking about you when I was, ah, dropping off supplies. Do you know where they moved the school pantry?"

"Over there, next to the parking lot." I showed her the room.

"*Merci*," she thanked me.

"*Pas de quoi.*" [no problem] I watched her head to the pantry and select several ready-made meals and three uniforms sets in different sizes. Curious, I watched the little girl enter the first grade class and check off supplies at the supply table. Since she had no supplies in her hands, she obviously was pretending to have them. I went to look at the name she had checked: Tanner Hebert. Same thing in the Kindergarten room. This time, Bailey Marie Hebert was the child with invisible supplies. *Curiouser and curiouser.* I stopped by Michelle's office to see if she knew the child. I knocked on her office door. "Are you busy?"

"Always. How can I help?" I walked over to her window and peeked out through the curtain.

"Do you see that child walking across the parking lot?" She moved in front of me to see. Now that teachers and parents were on campus, she'd switched from Rosie the Riveter attire to flowy floral and polka dotted dresses with big pockets in front.

Her curls were down but held back with big barrettes. God, her hair smelled good. What was that?

"Valerie Hebert, why?" Snickerdoodles! Her hair smelled of snickerdoodles. Distracted, I took another whiff.

"Beau, why?" she prodded.

Head in the game, Babineaux. "It's something ... My gut is telling me she's in trouble. She loaded up on food and school uniforms from the pantry. Plus, she signed for both a Tanner and a Bailey Marie Hebert, saying they had brought all their supplies, but there were no supplies."

"Not a problem. Let's see, she's in fourth grade." Michelle picked up a bag and wrote Valerie Hebert and Madame George on it. "Tanner is in first and Bailey Marie in Kinder." She wrote their names and teachers' names on two more bags. "Can you deliver these to the teachers?"

I grabbed up the bags. "Sure."

"You said she got uniforms from the pantry?" she asked.

"One set for each of them, I would guess."

"Please remind Madame George that Valerie needs another set of uniforms for her family. Please remind her to be discreet."

Heading out, I said, "Of course. Do you have a solution to every problem?"

"Education is problem solving. Speaking of problem solving. Once the teachers leave, can we meet and discuss the Open House? We will have logistical issues with parking and seating that we need to work out."

I nodded. "I'll be here. Around 4:00?"

"Perfect," she said and returned to her desk.

I grabbed the bags to deliver them to the teachers and Michelle went back to her organized chaos.

At 3:30, Etienne called. "Remember that graffiti I was checking on? Bad news, it is a gang symbol ... sort of."

"What do you mean, sort of?" I stopped on the sidewalk.

"It looks like someone copied it. They are trying to make it seem like it's Bandito territory, but they don't know how to tag."

"Why would anyone do that?"

"A kid trying to work his way into a gang, but they are very protective of their art. If I had to guess, I would say someone is trying to intimidate the school. Can you see if there are any issues? Nothing warrants an investigation, but my gut is telling me something is hinky."

"I'm meeting with Michelle in a half hour. I'll see if I can find out more." As I spoke with him, I closed and locked the gate to secure the school. I scanned the parking lot for any signs of danger. Thanks to Etienne, I was in protective mode.

"Michelle is it? When did you get on a first name basis?" Etienne teased.

"She asked me to call her that, smart aleck. Listen, I have to run. These teachers are trying to get everything set up on day one, and I'm the muscle to move all heavy objects."

"Must be tough."

"Shut up!" I snapped.

"Wanna go grab a beer after work? Perhaps a beer and a burger?"

I hesitated. "Maybe. Like I said, I'm meeting with Michelle at 4:00. I'm not sure how much time it takes to plan an Open House."

"Fine, but we are all hanging out this weekend. You can't miss because Armand is getting deployed again soon, and God knows when he'll be back."

"Tell me where and I'll be there." I scanned the perimeter as we finished our conversation.

"Well, let's do it at your house again. He is staying there anyway and you have plenty of crash space if any of us imbibe to excess."

"Imbibe to excess. You're such a nerd."

"Later asshole."

"Back at you!" I had to keep my calls PG on school grounds.

As I talked on the phone, little Valerie emerged again, this time with her younger siblings in tow. The little brother had Valerie's coloring, though it was difficult to discern through all the dirt. The little girl was what my mama called a Jolie Blonde, with blue eyes and blond hair in braids. Cute family. They were sitting at the picnic table eating. As I finished my conversation with Etienne, I went to the coke machine and bought three juice boxes.

"Here you go, kid." I handed the boxes to Valerie.

"We don't take charity," Valerie said, and then turned her back to me. I considered pointing out the pantry was charity, but decided that would be counterproductive.

"I thought they had orange juice in the machine. I tried three times, but every juice but orange came out. Apple and grape juice are not my favorites. You'd be doing me a favor if you made sure they did not go to waste."

Valerie looked at me suspiciously. "So this isn't charity?"

"Absolutely not, y'all are helping me." Valerie took the juice boxes and inserted the straws for her siblings.

"*Merci.*" The little girl with long blond braids and big blue eyes thanked me.

"Tanner!" Valerie nudged him. "What do we say?"

"I thought this wasn't charity, and we are helping him out," Tanner groused.

"Fair enough." I smiled. "Thank you for making sure the juice does not go to waste." Valerie nudged her brother again.

"Thank you for the juice," Tanner grumbled. I nodded to him and tipped my baseball cap. Cute kids.

8

An Annoying Intruder

Michelle

Beau Babineaux was a grumpy sweetheart. I watched the scene from my window and made a note not to divulge his secret soft underbelly. With a grin, I turned to the chaos of my office and sighed. "No rest for the weary. Calgon, take me away!"

"Who's Calgon?"

I jolted at the voice. "Weren't you were outside pretending to not like juice?"

"I finished my subterfuge and since we are meeting in ten minutes, I decided it was better to wait than be waited on." Beau walked into my office.

"Wait, I know that movie." My finger tapped against my temple as I tried to remember. "*Mistletoe and Menorahs*!"

Beau nodded. "My sister Angelle makes me watch it every year. It is my yearly Christmas torture. Then I make her hang out at the hardware store for an hour to even the score."

"You have strange holiday traditions in your family. We just open gifts, eat, and watch football and parades."

A snort, but no smile, and a snarky "weirdos" was Beau's response.

"You're right. What our holidays are missing is torture. Next Christmas, my sisters will be here copying, collating, and stapling my school fundraiser packets. God bless us, everyone" That time, his mouth twitched, for sure. *Victory*. "Give me a sec to clean up this chaos. The teachers' first week back is insane."

"No seriously Michelle, if you're overwhelmed or need time away, the Babineaux family camp is right through those woods." He pointed out my office window. "You can practically smell the campfire from here. It was one reason the position appealed to me. So close to my vacation spot."

A rustling noise sounded outside the office door.

"Hello, can I help you?" I called.

"*C'est moi*, Valerie. [It's me, Valerie] We just were seeing if you needed any help. We got stuff from the pantry and a set of uniforms, but ... uh ... Mama didn't have time or money to get us anymore, and we need two more sets. We can work for it. We don't take charity."

"Of course not. Let's find you something to do." When I held out my arm to her, she came over and gave me a side hug.

"Actually," Beau said, "I need tiny hands to tear up paper."

"Tear paper?" Valerie and I said simultaneously.

"Jinx," I said, and Valerie laughed. "Explain, *Monsieur (M.)* Beau."

"Renee made me help with a recycled paper art project. While I was cleaning all the classrooms, I put old papers in water to soak to prep for that same art project. The papers have dried and now I need help to cut up the papers into tiny pieces."

"There you go," I said. "Work with *M.* Beau on that project for an hour today and on Monday, then you can get two more uniforms each. Will that work?"

"Yes!" Valerie said excitedly.

Before she ran outside to tell her siblings, I reached in my pockets and got out three Hershey kisses. "*Un tit bec pour toi, ton frère, et ta soeur.*" [a little kiss for you and your siblings]

"*Merci madame!*" [Thanks ma'am] She skipped out of the room, chewing on her chocolate.

"Let me get them started and then we can talk." Beau followed her out.

Looking around my office, I heaved a sigh. "I have plenty to keep me busy in the interim."

Busy as I was, I couldn't resist watching Beau set up the paper tearing operation for the Heberts. This included more juice and snacks because paper tearing was hungry work. I ducked back into my office as Beau made his way back to our meeting.

"This might take a while. We'll log your overtime and, as always, the school provides food for overtime work." I pointed to the food delivery bags behind the door.

Ever enthusiastic about food, Beau asked, "What are we eating?"

"Brauddus burgers, I got yours with blue cheese. Is that ok?"

Beau rolled his eyes and clasped his hands to his chest. "Blue cheese is heaven. You don't get a lot of that in the Marines. Good call. Let's talk … open house." He grabbed his burger and took a big bite. While doctoring his ketchup with Tabasco sauce and between bites of his burger, Beau asked, "That's Friday before school starts, right? In two more weeks?"

"Yes, and there's a lot to plan." I ate my burger as well, dipping fries into his perfectly seasoned ketchup. The next two hours flew by as we discussed open house logistics. Halfway through the meeting, Valerie peered into the office. "Madame Michelle, it's getting late. We need to get home."

Beau pointed to the table. "Just leave the uncut paper in the dark bag and the cut paper in the white one."

"Do y'all need a ride home, Valerie?"

"No, Madame. My mama is walking to meet us," she said as she walked toward the door.

"You're sure?"

"*Oui, madame,*" [yes, ma'am] she called over her shoulder as she left.

"They okay?" Beau asked.

"I'm not sure." I searched for Ms. Hebert's contacts and called her number. Unfortunately, it went to voicemail, and I asked her to call me back. Then I glanced at Beau. "When they come to work on Monday, let's make sure all is well."

"A worry for another day?"

"A worry for another day, so back to the open house. Since it is a potluck, we'll need tables for food and for eating." After another hour we had finished discussing the open house details, from parking, to meeting room set-up, to babysitting locale. "Goodness, it is nearly 6:30. Go on home and we can talk tomorrow."

"I'll walk you to your car," Beau offered.

Shaking my head, I said, "I still have work to do."

"Then so do I. Call me when you're ready to leave." I rolled my eyes, but figured complaining was futile. He was a retired Marine, and I had mentioned security in the job description.

"Fine, I'll text you when I'm ready to go." Beau nodded and headed out to work on something, not sure what.

Finally, at ten pm, I texted Beau to let him know I was ready to leave.

"You sure do keep late hours." Beau walked with me to my car. From the shadows, a man stepped out. "Indeed, she does." Doug Blake, my ex, stepped between me and my car.

"Mr. Blake, this is private property. What are you doing here and so late at night?"

"Mr. Blake? We were married for two years, Michelle. You could call me Doug. And I could ask you the same. This is my property!" His coiffed hair and expensive suit might intimidate other people. But I had gone to school with him, I had married him, and I had slept with him, so I knew he was an idiot. Truthfully, he reminded me of Draco Malfoy, from Harry Potter, but less touchy-feely.

Under my breath, I added "Doug-ass" while pointing out, "This is my school." Beau's choked cough showed he heard me. "Just a reminder. The lease means you can't treat it like it's your own."

"As I've said before, I no longer want to lease the property to the school." He tried to tower over me, but Beau moved forward, protecting my space.

"And I told you we have an ironclad ten-year lease as we wait for the old high school to be restored. Donate to that project and speed it along, and you can get rid of us sooner." I moved a smidge closer to Beau.

"The place is a mess. What parents would want their students here? I'm surprised the board did not shut it down." Suddenly, Jeremy's ineptitude transformed into deliberate sabotage.

"See, this is why you shouldn't just sneak around at night like a vampire. Our wonderful new concierge fixed all the issues." I gestured to Beau.

Doug put his hands on his hips. "What about the graffiti? That was a gang tag."

Beau tsked. "Are you talking about the graffiti that I painted over two weeks ago? Actually, a deputy at the Sheriff's office researched it and found it was a dismal copy of a gang tag. Probably a pitiful attempt to intimidate someone. Tragic really. Such a piss poor attempt. An 'A' for creativity, but an 'F' for execution."

"Mr. Blake, as long as I am leasing this property, you need to give me a seventy-two hour warning of visits and inspections." I looked at Beau and fibbed. "Did you turn on the alarm and the security cameras?"

He did not miss a beat. "They are functioning perfectly. Set to call the sheriffs at a moment's notice. Also, my deputy friend will send a patrol here to pass throughout the night. We need to go now, Mr. Black, and as you are currently trespassing, I will need you to leave before we do."

"It's Mr. Blake," he said, his voice whiney, as he stomped towards his Range Rover parked behind a tangle of overgrown bushes.

"Looks like someone pissed in his Cheerios. Clearly a tantrum in the sandbox kinda kid." I snickered at that.

"God, what did I ever see in that loser? We probably should look into actually getting security cameras, but that should work for tonight." Beau opened my car door, and I got in and rolled down the window.

As he closed the door, Beau said, "I'll call my friend Etienne at the sheriff's office to let him know about the sketchy Mr. Blake's late-night visit. Another friend of mine, Marc Richard, runs a security company. Do you want me to give him a call?"

"Please, thank you. Ms. Clothilde mentioned him, but waiting on the board to fund security might take a while. Get me a quote and I'll see if I can just buy it myself."

9

Something's Up Buttercup

Michelle

Beau and I both arrived at school early on Monday. While I finished up welcome packets, he rearranged tables and chairs, preparing for the open house. When the Heberts arrived, around ten, he directed them to the table to finish cutting up the paper. When they finished cutting, they made a beeline to find me. Beau followed swiftly in their wake, to assign them more tasks so I could get back to work.

"*Nous sommes finis!*" Valerie said, having finished the task.With a dramatic gesture, I made the international symbol of choking and stuck out my tongue. "Oh non! You died?" Valerie snickered and fixed her error. "Funny Madame! I meant *Nous avons fini.*"

"*Très bien, va chercher vos uniformes.*" [Very good, go get your uniforms]

Valerie hesitated. "Is there anything else you need done? We ... I mean, Mama thinks we need one more uniform to keep from having to do laundry in the middle of the week. You know how busy she is." Valerie couldn't meet my eyes. Alarm bells went off in my head. Beau's eyes met mine; he felt it too. With my spidey senses tingling, I asked Beau, "Are there any other campus tasks for the Heberts?"

"Well, next Friday is the open house. There are a number of chairs and tables to arrange and rearrange. Can you help with that?"

"Yes, we can help with that," Valerie said, grinning.

I shook my head. "Tanner and Bailey Marie are too small. The Kindergarten teachers need the toys and playground balls washed for the Open House babysitting room. They could do that. Can you help before and after the open house?" Valerie nodded and looked relieved. With a smile, I changed the subject. "Excellent! Works for me, but for now, let's all break for lunch." Outside the office door were boxes from Dean-O's pizza. Valerie looked at the boxes with obvious longing. "I guess we will go home. *Bon appétit.*" She turned around, slumping her shoulders.

"You will do no such thing, young lady. When you work for the school, the school provides lunch. Go get Tanner and Bailey Marie," I said. The scent of Marie LeVeaux pizza filled the air as the Heberts joined us for lunch. "No seafood allergies, right?"

"Non, madame," they chorused. They dug into their pizza and between 'yumms' and bites of pizza, I worked my magic to find out what was going on with the Hebert kids.

"So, how is your mom?" I asked, taking a bite of pizza to give Valerie time to answer.

"Go, umm, going to miss the open house." Valerie hesitated. Something was definitely wrong.

"Oh no, well, we'll record our welcome message so she can watch it on our social media sites." The Queen of Nonchalance. I wiped my mouth with my napkin and ruffled Tanner's hair.

Valerie relaxed. "I'll let her know."

"Tanner, how did your summer go?" I took another bite. Nothing like silence to get kids talking.

"I didn't do nothin'," Tanner grumbled.

"*Pas rien*," I reiterated in French, encouraging them to use the language they've learned.

"*Rien*." Tanner reaffirmed and finished his first slice.

I grabbed another piece of pizza and added it to his plate. "So, your mother didn't send you to the free summer camps that we discussed?" He picked up the slice and shook his head. "Who took care of you while your mother worked this summer?" Silence. Aha … Beau's eyes met mine again, but he stayed silent because the art of getting kids to tell you what they don't want you to know was my domain.

"Well, we have to go. Thanks for the pizza." Valerie rose to beat a retreat and her siblings followed suit, except that Tanner was trying to balance three slices of pizza as he got to his feet.

"Just take the box," I said and turned to Beau. "I can't eat another bite, you?"

"Completely full. Take the box, Tanner." Tanner smiled and snagged the box. Beau reminded them, "Remember to come the rest of the week to help with toy cleaning and setting up everything for the Open House."

Valerie called over her shoulder as they scurried away, "We'll be here."

I waved at them and then turned to write reminders in my notebook.

"You want to tell me about that? Something is off."

Closing the notebook, I headed to the side office window and gestured for Beau to follow me. "Shhh —" We surreptitiously observed the Hebert's as they walked across the parking lot. Half-way to the road, Valerie scanned the school. Afterwards, she motioned for her siblings to run into the woods. Finger to my mouth, I quietly opened the back office window to see if we could eavesdrop on them as they walked through the woods.

"I'm tired," Bailey Marie whined.

"We'll be there soon," Valerie said.

Tanner asked, "For real. Can we go back home?"

"No, Mama didn't pay the bills."

Bailey Marie repeated, "I'm tired," her words barely audible.

Valerie reassured her. "I know, sweetie. We'll be there soon."

"Where is there?" Tanner grumbled.

Moments later, we couldn't hear them.

"That is not good, right?" Beau whispered to me.

"Right, something is off. I'll ask Janie, my secretary, to spend tomorrow contacting their mom. I think we have a situation." Grabbing my phone off my desk, I texted Janie.

Beau's gaze hadn't left the window. His attention focused on where their voices trailed off. "You want me to track them?"

"Track them?" I walked back over to the window.

He still didn't turn. "You know, follow their trail and see where they go."

"Yes, go now." I pushed him on the shoulder.

He turned to me and shook his head. "And leave you here alone for that Doug-ass person to come by … no. Once you leave, I'll track them."

"But they could be in danger. Also, I can't believe you heard his nickname."

"I have excellent hearing and tracking skills. So, go home and relax so I can track them." He told me, clenching his jaw and no doubt wanting to order me to go home. I debated for an instant. Despite having work to do, Beau was insistent on not leaving me alone at the school after our altercation with Doug-ass last night. Decision made, I grabbed a pile of work to take home and loaded up my tote. "Fine, just go now."

"Let me walk you to your car, and then I'll track them. Don't worry. I won't lose their trail."

10

Through the Woods

Beau

Once Michelle took off in her car, I hot-footed it into the woods. It took me less than ten minutes to realize where the trail was leading. I smiled. Valerie must have overheard my conversation about our family camp. The camp lights were on. I reconnoitered the area and peered in the window. Valerie was folding clothes, Tanner was on a step stool cleaning dishes, and Bailey Marie was wiping down the table.

Valerie ran the show. "C'mon y'all. We need to get to bed. Tomorrow we'll go back to school to earn those other uniforms."

"Do you think they will give us pizza again?" Tanner asked.

"Oh, I hope so. It was nice not having to fix dinner. Now get in your PJs, and we will have a family meeting to discuss tomorrow." Valerie reminded me of Michelle.

"With hot chocolate?" Bailey verified.

"With the last of the hot chocolate." The younger ones ran off and Valerie microwaved water for hot chocolate. With a mental note to pick up more hot chocolate for them, I moved away from the window to text Michelle.

> Found them. They're fine.

> Michelle: Where are they?!

> Staying in my family's camp. Valerie must have overhead me telling you about it.

> Michelle: Is their mother with them?

I scanned the camp.

> No, she's not here, & I have an unobstructed view. Just the kids.

> Michelle: She drives a beat up Hyundai, red I think.

I scanned again.

> There's no car here.

> Michelle: That's not good. Keep an eye on them while I call social services.

When I returned to the window, the kids sat around the table drinking hot chocolate.

"So after Friday," Valerie began, "we will have enough uniforms for the week, so we only need to wash on Saturdays. The dewberries and garden will give us enough fruit and vegetables, and we can get the rest of our food from the school pantry. Tomorrow we'll check out the camp to see if we can find anything more we can use. For now, we're safe."

"Can't we just let Madame Michelle know? She always helps everyone," Tanner asked.

Valerie shook her head. "She will have to turn us over to Social Services. You remember what happened to Max and his family? They split the kids up and sent them to foster care."

"I don't want to leave you," Bailey Marie said.

"Me neither. So keep our secret, and we will see how long we can stay here without anyone finding out. Now, put on your PJs, brush your teeth, and floss them. And remember, you don't have to floss all your teeth…"

"Just the ones you want to keep," they chorused.

"How long do you think it will be before Mama comes back?" Tanner asked.

Valerie hugged him. "Tanner, I don't know if she's coming back."

Ducking back into the shadows, I texted Michelle again.

No parent! Mom took off, and they don't know if she's coming back.

Michelle: Drat! Social services are not picking up. I've left them three messages already. I need to call the Sheriff.

Where would the Sheriff put them?

Michelle: In foster care.

They're safe here. I'll stand guard tonight & do a group text with my friend Etienne at the sheriff's office. They're comfortable and in bed.

Etienne, we have family at the school whose mom left her kids. The kids snuck in to my family camp. Dr. LeBlanc called social services & left three messages. Her next step is the Sheriff. The kids are comfortable and safe. Can I just watch over them tonight?

Etienne: Let me check with Sheriff Trahan.

A minute later, he responded,

Etienne: That works, but just to be on the up and up, I'll head out there too.

Park at the levee and walk, so you don't spook them.

Michelle: Thanks guys! Please follow them to school tomorrow. Then come by my office for breakfast, scotch eggs & sweet potato biscuits. You've both earned it!

A second personal text came in from Etienne.

Etienne: I like your new boss.

Me too. Bring me something to eat when you come.

Etienne and I watched the camp through the night. At around midnight, my phone vibrated with a new text message.

Michelle: How are they?

Serene and sleeping. No issues.

Michelle: Can I call you?

I'll call you. The phone ringing might scare them.

Signaling Etienne that I was going deeper into the woods to call, I dialed Michelle's number.

"Did they eat dinner?" She blurted out, with no greeting.

"Pretty sure that is what the pizza was, but you must have taught Valerie about nutrition, because they are using dewberries and the garden to get their fruits and veggies. They plan to use the pantry for the rest of their food."

"Did they say why their mom left?"

"No, but Valerie seems pretty certain that she won't be coming back." As we talked, I completed a patrol circuit.

"Gah! Adults suck!"

"Hey, we're both adults." Trees stood still, camp lights off, no movement detected.

"We are exceptions to the rule. Actually, their mom always seemed very devoted. There is no way Ms. Hebert would just leave them like that. *Pauvres bêtes,* [poor things] I was devastated was when my ex left and I didn't even like him that much."

I frowned. "Your ex was an idiot."

"No, he got what he wanted. To trade up for a younger model."

Rolling my eyes, I said, "Hah! More like traded down for a dumber model."

Michelle snorted. "I see you have met Stephie."

"Nope, I just haven't met many people smarter than you."

"Aww ... Anyway, that desertion wasn't a parent. I bet they're asking what they did wrong, what they could have done better. I don't understand. Val Hebert was struggling, but she was a wonderful mom and cared enough to keep her kids in a French immersion school. There have been no issues with the care of the children since Valerie began here five years ago. Something bad, bad happened." With a reverse of my patrol circuit, I headed back to camp. "I'll see if Etienne can find out anything about her."

"Thanks. Do you know anyone who fosters kids?"

I stopped. "My sister Angelle is a social worker. She and her husband, Alex Landry, foster kids. I'll call her now."

"It's too late!"

Shaking my head, I said, "Not for Gelly. She lives to help kids. I might even convince her to watch them at the camp so they don't have to move again."

"She would do that?"

I smiled, thinking of Gelly. "Are you kidding? She loves the camp. Let me see if she and Alex can meet us here tomorrow morning."

"Thank you! You're the best!"

"No problem." With that, I hung up the phone and immediately called Gelly.

"It is past midnight. This better be an emergency!" Gelly's roughened voice answered. I bit my lip. "Sorry, Gelly, it is an emergency. But everyone is healthy."

"Then what kind of emergency is it?" She was more alert now.

"You know how I started working for that school?" Nearing the end of my patrol, I scanned for danger as we spoke.

"Académie Immersion School, yeah, Dad told me."

"Well, this afternoon the school director, Dr. LeBlanc, noticed something was off with a family of kids."

I imagined her eyebrow rising. "Define off."

"They took a lot of food from the school pantry. They checked where their parents were supposed to check for supplies that they didn't have, and they asked to work for more uniforms. Then, after their work today, they darted into the woods. I tracked them to our camp and listened at the window. They are preparing to stay there for the long haul, and they don't think their Mother, who is their sole guardian, is coming back."

"Did Dr., what was her name again?"

"Michelle, Dr. LeBlanc." I imagined her in her overalls with her braids as I spoke.

"Did Dr. LeBlanc call social services?"

"She did and left them a few messages, but they're not picking up."

"Did she call the sheriff?"

My eyes darted to Etienne, who signaled for me to surveil the woods next to the camp. "Yes, Etienne is out here with me. We did not want to scare the kids, so we're guarding them tonight."

"Ok, I'm putting the paperwork in to foster them, so that social services will have it at the same time as they get Dr. LeBlanc's report. I'll meet you out there at seven am with breakfast for everyone and the paperwork in place. Hold on." Angelle whispered something to her husband, Alex. "Why don't we stay at the camp? It sounds like they are comfortable there and Alex and I have time off that we haven't taken this year."

"I was just going to ask if you could do that. Thanks Gelly. Best sister ever." I grinned.

"You're welcome, and I'm your only sister. Now, let me sleep."

"*Fais des beaux rêves*! [have beautiful dreams]" Walking around back, I scanned for movement.

"You too."

"Not tonight. Tonight, I'm on guard duty with Etienne." I returned to Etienne's side of camp prepared for late night guard duty.

V alerie woke the next morning to the smell of coffee and bacon. "Mom?!" she said, disoriented. "Mom!" She ran to the kitchen. Tanner and Bailey Marie were at the table talking to Gelly and Alex and eating pancakes, eggs, and bacon, while I was on the couch, drinking coffee.

"*Bon matin*, [Good morning] Valerie. Did you sleep well?" I asked.

"Don't split us up!" She shook her head, unable to catch her breath, and was looking pale. Before I could comfort Valerie, Gelly hurried over, knelt down, and spoke with her.

"Valerie, we aren't splitting you up. In fact, you don't even have to move. My name is Mrs. Angelle Landry, but everyone calls me Gelly. So you can call me, Ms. Gelly. I'm Beau's, Mr. Babineaux's sister, and I've already filled out the paperwork to foster your family together."

Tears welled in Valerie's eyes. "Together?"

"Yes, plus, since you're already in my camp."

"Our camp," I said from the couch.

"Our camp. Mr. Alex and I," she pointed to her husband, Alex, who was currently cutting up Bailey Marie's pancake, "are just going to move into the camp for a week. Until we figure out what to do."

"And then you'll split us up?" Valerie pulled back from her.

"No!" I said. "I promise you won't be split up. We will find a way, won't we, Gelly?"

"We will indeed." At that moment, Etienne walked in. When Valerie glimpsed his sheriff's uniform, she pokered up.

"Valerie, this is my friend, Mr. Etienne. He and I watched over you last night to make sure you were safe," I said, patting her tiny shoulder.

Valerie narrowed her eyes. "Are you going to split us up?"

Etienne shook his head. "No, absolutely not, but I am worried about your mama and so is Dr. LeBlanc. She said she's a wonderful mom and would never leave you."

"That's what I said," Tanner interjected from the table.

"She had a new boyfriend, Ray. Mama told someone on the phone that she was going to drop him. They went out about three weeks ago, and she hasn't come back."

"Three weeks, good lord! How have you been surviving?" Gelly asked as Etienne texted updates on his phone.

"We had just gotten groceries, so we used them all up. We had hurricane supplies that we went through. Mom had a money jar, and we used that to get more food. But then yesterday there was an eviction notice on our apartment door. Mama didn't pay the rent before she left." Gelly covered her mouth with her hand. Her eyes were glassy with unshed tears, but she didn't cry and instead nodded for Valerie to keep talking.

"Do you know Ray's last name? What did he look like?" Etienne asked.

"I don't. Mama just called him Ray. He was big." She gestured to show someone tall.

"Like Ultron big," Tanner said.

"Ultron?" came a few voices.

Etienne nodded, "I know Ultron, from the Avengers, right? So he had lots of muscles and he was tall."

"Um hum," Tanner nodded. "He looked more like Ironman though, with the same hair."

"Dark hair?"

"Um hum," Tanner nodded again.

"So, once you read the eviction notice, you went to the school?" Gelly asked her, trying to keep the story going.

"We were planning to go, anyway. We were out of money and needed the pantry for food and uniforms. Once I read the notice, I had everyone pack up essentials. I thought we might have to stay somewhere at the school, maybe in the bathroom or shed, but then I overheard M. Beau talk about his empty camp. I'm so sorry! Oh! Hold on!" She ran back to the bedroom and returned with a wad of cash.

"It is all there, all $700. I put an IOU under each mattress. We just thought we would need money."

A tear slipped down Angelle's cheek. "You found our emergency stash. You won't need that. We'll take care of you and, like my brother said, you'll stay together, I promise. Now, come and eat breakfast."

Out of nowhere, Valerie ran over to me and hugged me tight. "Your shoulders have been supporting a lot of weight lately, huh, Valerie?" She nodded as she cried. "C'mon, if you're anything like Madame Michelle, and I think you are, you need to eat regularly."

"They both get grumpy when they're hungry," Tanner said helpfully.

After a few rounds of 'Do not/ Do too,' they began to eat breakfast.

With a nod to Gelly, I returned to the couch to text Michelle. "I let Madame Michelle know that all is well and that you are safe and sound. She was worried about you." Valerie nodded, no doubt, because that is what Madame Michelle did. She fretted over everyone. "Also, please call me M. Beau. You can call my sheriff friend over there, Mr. or M. Etienne."

Etienne and I were standing at the doorway, fixin' to leave, but we made Gelly promise that they would walk the Littles, which we started calling them, to school. Actually, we first tried to convince them they did not need to go, but Valerie insisted.

"We gave you our word and Hebert's don't go back on their word."

"Everyone knows that," Tanner nodded.

Valerie added, "Our mama raised us right."

Before we headed out, Etienne had one more question. "Valerie, what's your mama's first name?"

Tears welled in her eyes. "Valerie, like me. She said the first-born girl of the first-born girl is always named Valerie."

"That's a nice tradition," Etienne's eyes met mine.

Something was off. As we walked to Etienne's sheriff's car. He was talking fast into his phone. "Any news on Ray with dark hair and a body like Ultron? Also, I need to file a missing person report on Valerie Hebert, last seen three weeks ago with Ultron Ray." Etienne disconnected. "I'll let you know when we hear anything. C'mon Beau, I'll drop you off at school."

"No, Michelle got us breakfast. That means she wants an update from both of us. Plus, scotch eggs and sweet potato biscuits!" Rubbing my hands together in anticipation of the meal, I ducked into his car.

Etienne got in and we started down the drive. "She really knows how to get people to show up for meetings, doesn't she?"

"That she does." I stared across the woods, wondering if Michelle could help us figure everything out. She was a very ... capable woman.

11

Pre and Post Open House

Michelle

On the table, I had arranged Scotch eggs and sweet potato biscuits, accompanied by cups, plates, napkins, coffee pods, half and half, and sugar. My fancy coffee pot was ready as well.

When Beau and Deputy Benoit stepped into the meeting room, I extended my hand to the deputy. "Bonjour. I'm Dr. Michelle LeBlanc, school director." Deputy Benoit shook my hand. "Nice to meet you. Deputy Etienne Benoit here. Beau and I are close friends." He swiped up a Scotch egg. "Nice spread."

"The better to convince you to tell me everything. So, how are the Heberts this morning?" I asked, handing out cups of coffee as the men sat at my meeting table.

"My sister, Angelle, we call her Gelly, and her husband Alex Landry are fostering them. They'll stay at the camp with them for at least a week until we find a more permanent solution." Beau took a sip and grabbed a biscuit.

The steam from my third cup of coffee swirled in the sunlight as I sipped. "And Mrs. Hebert?"

"Went out with her boyfriend, who she planned to dump three weeks ago and never returned." Etienne said between bites.

"Oh my God, three weeks. Those poor children."

"They're pretty self-sufficient." Beau nodded, finishing his biscuit and grabbing another. "These biscuits are my favorite."

Smiling, because that's why I bought them. I walked to the window and sighed. "Mrs. Hebert worked several jobs, so they always had to be pretty responsible."

"Luckily, for Tanner and Bailey Marie, they have a very responsible sister, and she's a hard worker." Beau came up behind me and put his hand, covered in powdered sugar, on my shoulder as we watched his sister and brother-in-law emerge from the woods with the Heberts.

"Valerie is a 40-year-old in a 9-year-old's body." I sighed as I watched them.

Etienne cleared his throat. "But they still need their mom, and I am working on that. We filed a missing person report and have a BOLO on her boyfriend, Ray. Any chance you know his last name?" Turning, I saw Etienne's eyes darting between Beau's hand resting on my shoulder and the food he was devouring. Clearing my throat, I stepped back from Beau and the window. "I don't, but I will see if any of the parents do, at the open house."

Etienne smirked at Beau, donned his sheriff's cowboy hat, and promised to text back once he received any updates.

The younger Heberts spent the rest of the week cleaning toys and playground equipment. Valerie helped Beau to arrange chairs for general meeting and in each classroom, ensuring the parents had adult-sized seating when they visited their child's teachers.

Petty cash provided pizza and salad for anyone helping get the school ready for the open house. This time from Pizza Village, plus I ordered salad since God knows how long it had been since the Heberts had eaten healthy meals. Pizza Village's salad was so delish everyone ate it. Beau walked the Littles to camp each afternoon so Gelly, as I was coming to know her, could watch them, and we could finish our work.

The night of the open house, as I did for every parent meeting, we had French Immersion high school students babysit any children that came. After dropping off the Heberts, Beau offered assistance to anyone who needed it. The open house progressed without incident. After the assembly, I asked anyone who was friends with Ms. Valerie Hebert to please see me after the meeting. When the rest of the parents went to their respective classrooms, Beau and I met with Ms. Hebert's friends.

"Thank you for meeting with us. We learned just recently that Ms. Hebert disappeared over three weeks ago, after a date with her boyfriend, Ray."

"Oh my, what about her kids?!" Mrs. Istre asked, her hands clasping together.

Beau's voice was reassuring. "They are fine. My sister is fostering them. We are more worried about Ms. Hebert. From what I have learned, she would never have left her kids alone, especially not for that amount of time."

"She would not." Mrs. Young shook her head.

"Do either of you have any information about the boyfriend, Ray?" I asked.

"He was *pas bon*; [no good] he hit Val. That's why she was breaking up with him," Mrs. Young said, and Mrs. Istre nodded.

"What about his last name or where he worked? Maybe what he did for a living?" Beau asked.

"Perhaps he worked off shore? When they first started going out, Val said that she was glad he had his two weeks off." Beau texted an update to Etienne.

"Do you need any help in fostering the kids?" Mrs. Young asked. "I could take the baby, Bailey Marie. She is such a sweetie." She smiled.

"No, no, one reason the kids did not report their mom missing was because they were afraid they would be split up. We are keeping them together," I said.

The ladies nodded and then headed to their children's classes for the open house. As the meeting room door closed behind Valerie Hebert's friends, I said, "Well, we learned something."

Beau's brow furrowed. "Let's hope that's enough."

After the open house, the Heberts helped Beau put away toys and chairs, as I worked in my office. While finalizing last minute issues with the schedules, someone knocked on my door.

"Come in," I said, focused on my work; assuming it was Beau and or the Heberts.

"You had quite a few parents for your open house. I can see why you want to hold on to the lease. You must be making a fortune off all the tuition money from those parents." My ex, Doug, said, entering the room and closing the door behind him.

"First, Mr. Blake, what are you doing here? Second, we're a public school. The parents don't pay tuition. The money we do get from the state goes back into the school." I moved from the meeting table to my desk to put distance and an obstacle between us.

"I was thinking that perhaps, to break that lease, you needed a little more personal persuasion. We should go out. A steak dinner, some dancing, and, you know, fun. To show you, I'm just a good guy. You married me, after all. Let me break that long, dry streak you've been having."

A snort escaped from me, uncontrollable and spontaneous. "You're not a good guy. That's why I divorced you. Plus, you're clueless to boot. If you were a good guy, you would know that coming into my office late at night, shutting the door, and propositioning me makes you automatically a creep. Plus, you're married, so you're a creepy creep. Now leave."

"I don't think so," Doug said, moving forward and grabbing my arm across the desk.

Pulling back, I asked, "Planning to use rape to break the lease, Doug? Let go of me. You're an idiot."

"Let's see if you think so after this." He dragged me over the desk and smashed his lips down on mine. At that instant, the door slammed open. While the sound distracted Doug, I punched him as hard as I could in the eye. Crap that hurt my hand.

"God dammit, what did you do that for?" he yelled.

"Because you are gross and you can't just kiss people without asking. Where's my mouthwash?" I ransacked my desk drawers for my stash of travel mouthwash. When I located it, I opened it and glugged half the bottle. As I swished mouthwash around my mouth, I turned on the voice recorder app on my phone using my watch.

"Geeet !" I gargled and pointed to the door.

"What?" Doug pretended he couldn't understand.

"She said get out and if you come back on the property, we're pressing charges for assault." Beau stood stoic at the doorway with his arms crossed over his chest and his eyes laser focused on my now squirming ex.

"This is my property and I can come and go as I please. Plus, Michelle wanted me to kiss her. This whole dance is about her wanting me back," Doug stated, with a straight face, no less.

Mouthwash spray from my mouth as I chortled. "You're delusional. You gross me out. What was I thinking marrying you? I've been putting up with you because you inherited the property from your sweet grandfather, but I don't have to like it. There is no way I'm interested in getting back with you in any way, shape, or form. Now get out of here!"

"This is my property!" Doug yelled as he used his pocket square to soak up the spray of mouthwash.

"Fine." I pulled out my cell and dialed Etienne.

"Etienne, I've just been assaulted in my office. Beau is a witness. My ex husband, Doug Blake, grabbed me, dragged me across my desk, and kissed me without my permission. Now he's saying I wanted it and he won't leave. He says it is his property and he can come on the school campus whenever he wants. Yes, I have a legal lease for ten years. Un, huh? OK, perfect. See you soon."

I smiled at Beau. "He's on his way."

Doug tried to escape, but Beau blocked the door. "Now, just a minute. I think there has been some kind of misunderstanding here."

Beau uncrossed his arms and pounded his fists together. "No, from what I heard and witnessed, you are pretty much the asshole in this situation."

"A ten-year rent-free lease that is only on year five. That is not a lease. I either get the property or I get my pound of flesh. You have some pounds to give, Mrs. Blake."

I gagged. "Sorry, I just threw up a little in my mouth. Now, hear this, creepy Mr. Blake, my name is Dr. LeBlanc." I emphasized the Doctor because it annoyed him and to be a bitch. "I never took your name, if you will remember, and I certainly don't go by it now. Furthermore, the lease you hate is legal and binding. I have a slew of attorney parents that would be more than willing to explain it to you. And finally, what you just said is illegal and blackmail and..." I held up my phone, "is now recorded." I put the phone behind my back as Doug grabbed for it, tearing my shirt instead. "The app already uploaded a copy to my cloud. You, dumbass, you're screwed."

"That's enough of that." And with that, Beau grabbed Doug by the back of his shirt and carried him away from me.

"Let go of me. This is assault." Doug squirmed.

"It's probably because you tried to grab Mme. Michelle and tore her shirt. You shouldn't do that. It is not nice. *Pas bon*," came a voice from the doorway. We turned to see Valerie hovering there.

"Exactly! Thank you, sweetie. Can you go by the gate and open it for Deputy Etienne? He should be here soon."

"*Oui madame*." [Yes ma'am] Valerie headed out.

When Etienne arrived, he took custody of Doug and put him in handcuffs.

"I'm sending you the recording of him telling me I have to break the lease or he gets his pound of flesh out of me."

Etienne cringed. "Gross. You're a creep." Etienne shoved him in the squad car, slammed the door, and nodded at me. "Nice job divorcing him."

"Thank you. I thought so as well. Also, Beau and our little friend over there will testify that he assaulted me twice. He is the one that ripped my shirt. I want a restraining order against him. Until the lease is up and we vacate the property, I don't want him anywhere near our school."

"I'll get right on that." Once Doug was in the back of the sheriff's car, Angelle and Alex zoomed up in their green Subaru.

I tilted my head quizzically at Beau. "I called them. You're going to need to decompress after this and they can watch the Littles." He motioned his head towards the schools where the Heberts were peeking out a window.

"Wait to get the kids," I whispered when they rushed up to me. "I don't want Doug to pay them any attention. He would use them as leverage to cause problems." Angelle nodded and she, Alex, and Beau formed a barrier between the school and Doug, a wall of disdain for him. From the corner of my eye, I spotted Valerie still peeking out the window. Doug's stare made her pull back. Crap, I thought.

12

Can She Make a Roux?

Beau

Once he had taken off, Etienne called me from the car. "The tow truck is on its way to retrieve the perp's Range Rover."

In the background, Doug-ass griped, "I'm not a perp, and that car is three times your yearly salary, so who's the loser?"

"*Je vas passer par Opelousas* .[I'm going to go by way of Opelousas] *Je passerai te voir après*." [I'll pass by to see you after] We both chuckled, fully aware the detour would add an hour to the route. No way for Doug to call his lawyer and stop his car from being impounded. Plus, it gave the Krewe a chance to transport the Heberts safely away.

After ending the call, I turned to Gelly. "Let's get the kids together and head to the camp. Gelly, he saw you. We have to assume he'll retaliate against both Michelle and you."

"And you, Beau," Michelle said.

"Naw, he's a coward. He will only retaliate against someone he thinks is weaker than he is. He's a bully."

"Let's get the kids and head to the camp," Alex said. They loaded the Heberts into the Subaru and drove them back to the camp.

"It sure is a lot faster if we walk," Tanner said.

"Yes, but sometimes it is safer to drive," Gelly told him.

Once they arrived at the camp, Michelle gave all three of them a big hug. When Michelle tried to let go, Valerie's grip tightened, and she refused to release her. "He is going to try to hurt you, Madame. It's in his eyes. He has eyes like Ray."

Michelle comforted Valerie by patting her back, assuring her, "I'll be fine."

Valerie shook her head against Michelle's shoulder. "That's what Mama said."

"Don't worry, I'll take care of her," I said, and Valerie relaxed, marginally, with that statement and let Michelle go.

"Can you stay here with us? Can M. Beau and M. Etienne stay too? You don't want us to worry, do you?" Valerie asked.

Gelly giggled at Valerie's obvious manipulation. "It will be like a sleepover! That sounds like fun!" At Ms. Gelly's words, Valerie's smiling eyes met hers.

"Could we, just for the weekend?" She flashed her big brown eyes and Michelle hesitated. Powerless against the sad eyes, she relented. "Fine, but I don't have pajamas or clothes for Monday, and it is the first day of school."

"Let me personally escort you home, so you can gather your things," I offered.

Michelle held up both hands. "I can head over by myself. I'm a big girl."

"But Mr. Blake might get you," Valerie said. "He looked really mad at you when Deputy Etienne drove off with him." With that, I realized Doug had noticed Valerie before he was driven off. A problem for another day. The primary goal tonight was to ease the Heberts' worries.

"Fine, M. Beau can accompany me." She hugged the Heberts and then tried to hop into my jacked up truck.

"Need a hand?" I asked, but before she could respond, I lifted her by the waist into the vehicle.

"While I once might have questioned the necessity of a jacked up truck, my perspective has changed since the flood. After losing my house, I'm now thankful that we have trucks like these."

"Good to know that I have some uses." With that, I closed her door and rounded the truck to climb in. As I started up Big Betsy, Michelle's hand gently touched mine. "I didn't get to thank you. For coming in and taking Doug-ass in hand. He really is a pest. His grandfather is probably turning in his grave."

"Yep, *pourri-gaté*. [spoiled rotten] What did you ever see in him? Can I ask? Also, where am I headed?"

"The Dougtastrophe is a long story. Maybe later. You're headed to Arnaudville. Since the flood, I've been renting the apartment over my parent's garage."

"Excellent, I get to meet the 'rents'." I headed to Highway LA 31. With very clear and concise directions (teachers should write all directions), we arrived at Michelle's parents' house. A woman who could only be Michelle's mama worked in the moonlit garden.

"What are you doing out here? And in the dark?" Michelle asked her mom.

"Michelle Lynn LeBlanc, is that any kind of tone to take with me?" the woman scolded. "Now introduce me to your nice young man." She batted her eyes at me. I believe I gave her a deer in headlights expression in response.

"Beau Babineaux, this is my mom, Ellie Mae LeBlanc."

Ellie Mae, an older version of Michelle with the opposite coloring, had the same compact, curvy body, and facial structure. But this version had bouffant blond hair and enormous blue eyes. *A glimpse of your future*. Woah! Hold on,

I needed to rein in those thoughts. Not only was Michelle my boss, but I needed to protect her, and not imitate Doug's idiotic possessive behavior.

"Mom, this is Beau. He's our concierge at the school, and he has also been keeping us safe."

"That's nice," Ms. Ellie Mae intoned, clearly not listening. She shook my hand and asked, "So, Beau, who's your mama?"

"Can you make a roux?" Michelle said, snickering at the stereotypical Cajun get-to-know-you greeting.

"I can make a roux and my mama is Denise Babineaux, from Scott, more specifically, the Marais Bouleur area." I shook her hand. A hand nearly the same size as Michelle's.

She tilted her head. "*Alors tu parles français?*" [So you speak French]

I nodded. "*Depuis mon enfance.*" [Since I was a child]

Ms. Ellie Mae gave a firm nod of approval. "He's a keeper."

Michelle rolled her eyes. "He's an employee, a fabulous one, and a friend. Mom, stay here and entertain him, will you, while I pick up some clothes?"

"God knows you don't want him to see your mess of an apartment. Hand to God, that girl will drown in paperwork one day!" Ms. Ellie Mae called after her.

"Thanks mom! And on that note, I will make my escape." She ran up the steps to her garage apartment. Once she got to her apartment, she kept the door ajar, no doubt, in case I needed a quick rescue. Let the third degree begin.

"Only," Ms. Ellie Mae said, "You don't want to just be an employee and a friend."

"Ah, ahem, can I help you here?" I asked and grabbed up her basket.

"Smooth," she teased. "Yes, you can help me gather the filé. It is the first full moon of August."

"You planning to make gumbo soon? Seems a little warm for that."

"Filé must be dried out and saved for the first cold front gumbo. I'll invite you." She cut leaves and placed them in my basket.

I tried to make small talk. "That's mighty kind of you. So, did you teach Michelle her French?"

"Actually no, we got in trouble for speaking French at school, and we wanted to save her from that, so she only spoke English. She studied French on her own. When she became a teacher, she got a scholarship, one of her many scholarships, to study in a French immersion program in Nova Scotia. Bruce, honey, where did Shell study in Nova Scotia?" she yelled toward the front porch.

"Ste Anne University, dear!" he yelled back.

"Came back speaking French and, well, you probably already know she's a firecracker. She got her degrees so she could run a school. And now she is, because what Michelle LeBlanc wants, Michelle LeBlanc gets."

Nodding, I said, "I've noticed that about her."

"I bet you have noticed other things as well." Quickly changing the subject as the expert gossip she was, Ms. Ellie Mae asked, "Denise Babineaux, what was her maiden name?" She finished cutting and held her hand out for the basket.

Shaking my head, I carried it to the porch for her. "Don't laugh, but it was Babineaux, no relation or at least not a super close one."

She did laugh. "Not a problem. There are even closer relations in our own family." She tipped her chin, asking me to come closer and whispered, "First cousins."

"No!" I feigned shock.

She chuckled. "*C'est la verité.* [It's true] That, however, was a long time ago, my great-grandparents. What's your Daddy's name?"

"Herman." I handed over the basket to her.

Ms. Ellie Mae called in to her house, "Bruce, honey, do we know a Denise or a Herman Babineaux from the Scott area?"

Mr. Bruce came out the screen door and onto the porch. "I know a Herman that works on my car at the auto repair shop on Cameron Street, on the way to Scott. He's a car genius. Any relation?"

I nodded. "That's my dad. He's been working there for years. He runs the farm, but he loves fixing cars, so he and his buddy opened a shop."

She handed her basket to Mr. Bruce. "So you come from good, hardworking people. This clearly is not your first job. What did you do before you started working for my sweetie?"

"Marines ma'am for twenty years, since I graduated from high school."

Ms. Ellie Mae beamed at me. "So, you have a pension, but you're still working."

I straightened my shoulders. "Have to work, Ma'am. The choice was on my daddy's farm or on my own terms, and I've always done things on my own terms. Plus, it's a really wonderful school. I enjoy working there."

"It's a successful school. Something for my Shell to be proud of."

"Shell?"

"Our little nickname for her." Ms. Ellie Mae said, as she handed her work gloves to her husband. "So tell me about your family."

"It is just my mom, Denise, my dad, Herman, and Gelly. My older brother, Théo, was a Marine as well, but he was killed in action."

Her hand rested on her heart. "Oh, I'm so sorry."

I turned to stare out into their garden. "It's alright. It has been a while."

Ms. Ellie Mae came up behind me and put her hand on my shoulder. "Time doesn't make grief easier, it just makes your world bigger, so you're not constantly rubbing against that grief. It always hurts the same."

I nodded. "Yes, yes, that is so true. It helped that I could focus on taking care of my baby sister, Angelle. We call her Gelly. We're staying with her tonight. She is fostering the children."

"Children?" She gestured for me to sit in one of the porch rocking chairs.

After selecting a rocker, I explained the whole situation. "The Heberts, we just learned their mama left weeks ago on a date and did not come back. Michelle—"

"—Shell," she interrupted as Mr. Bruce joined her on the porch swing.

"Shell figured out something was off. I tracked them through the woods to my family's camp." I explained what had happened. "So, we are all spending the night ... like a sleepover."

Ms. Ellie Mae's eyebrow raised. "Glad to know you are not taking my Shell for an evening of illicit love."

Before I could sputter a response, Michelle, Shell, returned. "Oh good God, mother!" On that, she scurried down the stairs. It was clearly time to rescue me.

"Ah, you're back. I was wondering if you had just collapsed in exhaustion on your bed." She turned to me. "She's a very hard worker."

I hid my smile. "So I've noticed."

"Mother, we are staying with three kids from school, because—"

"Yes, yes, Beau explained everything to me. Oh, the poor babies! Bruce!" She turned to her husband. "Get me that Angel Food cake. You will give them that to eat tonight. It will make them feel better."

"Honey! I haven't even had a piece."

"Don't whine, I'll make you another one." Mr. Bruce went to get the cake.

"While your daddy is getting the cake, you can explain to me why do they need you two there? If Beau's sister and her husband are staying with the little ones, why do they need you?"

Michelle hesitated, but I did not. "Michelle, Shell, was attacked tonight."

She elbowed me. "Don't say attacked. You're going to scare her."

"Doug Blake, her ex, grabbed her, yanked her across her desk and forced a kiss on her. Then, he tried to yank her phone out of her hands, ripping her shirt. He's a menace."

Ms. Ellie Mae shook her head. "That boy was always bad news. His mama spoiled him. God knows what you ever saw in him."

"Oh yay, the lecture on my poor life choices. Can't get enough of that one."

"I'm going to let that sass slide because apparently you've had a scare. However, I will just say that I can't believe Doug-ass — Isn't that was your sweet Aurelie calls him?" I started fake coughing and Ms. Ellie Mae grinned at me and continued, "I can't believe Doug-ass' Pawpaw left him everything. Remember how much Pawpaw Blake used to talk about his niece's family? They would visit him in the nursing home sometimes when you went to read to him."

"Read to him?" I asked.

"Yes, Shell would practice her French by reading to the French-speaking nursing home residents. They loved her. She still does it every other Sunday, don't you, dear?"

"Yes, mother, is there anything else you would like to tell Beau before we leave?"

Ms. Ellie Mae handed me her phone. "Put your number in here. If I think of something, I'll text it to you."

Michelle, Shell, put her forehead in her hands. "Kill me now!"

Suppressing a smile, I inputted my number into Ms. Ellie Mae's phone. After which, Mr. Bruce handed me the Angel food cake along with a container of cool whip and garden fresh strawberries.

"Thanks Daddy!" Michelle smiled up at him.

"You stay safe," he said to her and then he looked into my eyes, "and you keep her safe."

"Yes, sir. You two have a restful night. It was nice meeting you." I shook his hand and Ms. Ellie Mae gave me a hug.

As we walked away, her mama said *sotto voce*, "Promising, very promising indeed."

13

Slumber Party

Beau

"Your mom is a pistol." I started up the truck. "She's very energetic, like you."

Shell leaned back in her seat. "She's a nut, but I love her. She was my rock when Doug left. It was chaos, and then the flood happened, so anything I'd salvaged from the divorce was washed away."

"Decluttering by God?"

She chuckled. "Yeah, actually, it gave me a fresh start. Imagine, I come home from five weeks abroad to learn French, and my husband is in bed with some floozy. He was so lonely without me. Which is what he said, but the private investigator that my parents hired, Tommy Ashy, you know him?"

"Know … somewhat … related to the building supply Ashys?" Turning onto Highway LA 31, I headed towards the camp.

"Tangentially, anyway, Tommy uncovered he had started the affair at the beginning of our marriage. He just needed me to pay half the bills. Anyway, I got a killer lawyer, and I got the house and no alimony."

I frowned. "I thought the guy paid alimony."

"Traditionally, but usually the big bread earner pays."

"Hold on." This conversation was distracting me, so I pulled into the Poche's parking lot and turned to her. "Explain. Weren't you a public school teacher then? How would you be the big bread earner? Renee can't even afford to drink beer at a decent establishment. She's poor."

"Doug-ass was 'between jobs'." Shell air quoted.

"So not just a dumbass, a lazy dumbass."

"Yes, he thought he could get alimony because he said he 'supported me'." She air quoted again. "Apparently, he hadn't grasped the concept of bank records."

"Sorry to be judgmental, but how were you married to such a loser?"

Shell turned away from me. "Meh, he was pretty and after high school and in college, I was very self-conscious about my weight. Having someone want me made me happy."

I scanned her from head to toe. The curls, the curves, the dress, the pumps. She was a knockout. "You're perfect, a pocket-size Venus. What are you talking about?"

"Actually, I was slimmer and fitter in college. It was more a 'body dysmorphia' thing. Doug took advantage, and we had one year of wedded hell and one year of waiting for a divorce before sweet liberty."

"Good riddance." Nodding, I started the truck and merged back onto the highway.

Shell relaxed. "Absolutely. Since I shed Doug-ass, my life has turned around. I got my Master's and my doctorate, and best of all, I got my baby, the Académie Immersion school. All in all, life is grand."

Turning towards the camp, I asked, "So why is Doug-ass still in your life?"

"His arrogance and my bad luck? I went to school with Doug. He was always Mr. Popular, less for his personality and more because he provided free liquor at parties. His mother thought he could do no wrong, and the teachers couldn't complain because his parents gave generously to the school. He doesn't exactly know how to take 'no' for an answer."

"So he's used to being admired and getting his way." I nodded. "And now he has your lease?"

"Yes, that's where the bad luck comes in. It's weird because when I would go to read in French to Pawpaw Blake in the nursing home, he hated Doug. He discussed his nieces and nephews and how he wanted to take care of them, but never Doug-ass."

"Can you send me Tommy's contacts?" I asked, turning off the highway onto a secluded side road that led to the camp.

"Why?"

"I want him to send his info to Etienne. Something's afoot; I smell a rat." As I thought about it, I made a mental note to ask Etienne to have a chat with Mr. Ashy.

"Then Doug can't be far away because he is the rattiest rat. What about you?"

"What about me?" When I glanced at her, her focus was on me.

"What's your story?"

Shrugging my shoulders, I said, "Not much of a story. When I was seventeen, my big brother Théo died on a mission. He was a Marine Recon. We don't know where he was or what he was doing, but my parents received a folded flag, a handful of shells, and a gold star."

Shell tried to hide her face as she brushed away a tear. "So you enlisted?" she asked, her voice cracking.

"I was planning to anyway, but I was more motivated once I got in." As I gazed at the road ahead, my mind wandered, reflecting on my life. I shook my head. "Anyway, I spent twenty years fighting the bastards, and then I took my pension and left."

She snorted. "Sounds like Seinfeld's 'yadda yadda yadda'."

"I don't get the reference, remember I've been fighting for twenty years. I may not get all your cultural references."

"It was before your time, a re-run I used to watch. Anyway, to explain away difficult or embarrassing things, they would say 'yadda yadda yadda,' Like I joined the Marines, yadda, yadda, yadda, and then I collected my pension."

"Well, some of the yadda is classified."

"Understood." We were silent for the rest of the drive.

After parking, I turned to her. "No marriages or engagements, and the few girlfriends I've had ended the relationship when they transitioned back to civilian life. All I've ever done is to be a Marine, visit my family, and send money home to my parents."

"Aw, you supported them. That's so sweet." She beamed at me.

"Well, ah, I thought that was what I was doing. But apparently, my dad, besides being a successful farmer and a hobby mechanic, also plays at the stock market. Instead of using my money for essentials, which he insists he will always provide, he put it in the stock market. Made a pretty penny, too."

She grinned. "So, you're a rich janitor?"

"I'm not a janitor, remember? I'm a concierge."

She nodded at that. "Indeed, you are." And then suddenly she leaned over, gave me a kiss on my cheek, and hopped out of the truck. Her short little legs did not make it to the ground, and she tripped, falling on her butt. "Dang it, that would have been a perfect exit scene."

"It worked for me!" Walking around Big Betsy, I picked her up and looked at her backside, which was covered in mud. I pressed my lips together. "You're gonna need to change your clothes."

She tried to turn to look at her backside, but couldn't, so she used her hand to try to brush off the dirt. "Ugh, mud. I didn't think it was that wet."

"Welcome to camp life." I grabbed her overnight bag off her shoulder, my go bag from the back of the truck, and headed to the camp.

The moment we walked in the door, all three Heberts called out in unison, "Slumber party!"

"You betcha!" Shell responded. "Just let me change into my PJs."

As she headed to her room, Tanner stage whispered, "Does Madame Michelle know she sat in mud?" Gelly and Alex laughed.

The slumber party was an unqualified success. First, we he-men worked to build a roaring fire so we could cook and to keep the mosquitos at bay.

"What's that?" Tanner asked when we took our flint and steel fire starters.

"Fire starters," I said, trying to light the tinder.

"Can I try?"

I shook my head. "Not tonight Tanner. We need more safety measures in place if we are going to be training you." Tanner took it philosophically. We didn't say we wouldn't show him, just not now.

Alex and I did show the Littles, as I thought of them now, how to roast hot dogs over an open fire with sticks from the surrounding woods. Then, for dessert, we modeled how to roast marshmallows and make s'mores. We sang *La porte en arrière* [The Back Door] and *Pauvre Tit' Johnny* [Poor Little Johnny] that the Littles had learned in school. We even pulled out the family corn hole game and played a few rounds.

"Is there such a thing as a corn hole shark?" The moment I spoke, all eyes focused on Shell.

"What? I've played this game my whole life. *C'est en forgeant qu'on devient forgeron.*" [practice makes perfect] She shrugged and then sank the next three bean bags in the hole.

After Shell whooped us, it was bedtime. The Littles took showers and brushed their teeth so Gelly could read to them in English and Shell in French before they went to sleep. Once the kids were sound asleep, the ladies joined us on the screened-in porch, sipping on hot chocolate while we enjoyed our refreshing LA31 beers. To relax we had the ubiquitous two Cajun rockers and a porch swing. Gelly and Alex each took a rocker, Shell sat on the swing, and I took a seat next to her. While we were drinking our libations, Etienne drove up and greeted us. "*Comment les affaires?* "[How is it going?]

"*Ça se plume.*" [It's going] I responded. Then Etienne turned to Shell. "I have a present for you."

"Ew! I love presents." Shell beamed.

"Hey!" I said reflexively. Shell shrugged her shoulders while everyone else just smirked.

"Relax, it is not what you think," he said and handed Shell a paper.

"Oh, my very own restraining order. Just what I always wanted!" Shell batted her eyes at him.

"I do what I can to make all the women happy."

"With restraining orders?" Gelly jibed.

"What a girl wants. We all work within our skill sets. Now for the bad news. Within ten minutes of Doug being booked, his lawyer was there and because it was Doug Blake of the Blake family, he was out on bond by seven pm."

"Early enough to have followed us back to the camp." I deduced.

"Yep, so I will stay the night like last night and y'all can get some sleep."

"We'll take turns on watch. I'll take the first shift until midnight, then Alex, then Etienne. Does that work for y'all?"

"Works for me. Where can I sleep? It has been a long day and a half." Shell showed Etienne the men's sleeping bunks and then headed back to the screened-in porch to finish her hot chocolate and swing on the porch swing with me.

"So, how long have you two been married?" She asked Gelly and Alex.

"We've been together fifteen years, but only married for ten of them." Alex said.

"Wow! Married right after high school."

"Well, we dated throughout high school and married in my first year of college. Alex was working off shore by then, working on his degree online, and I got sick, so I needed health insurance."

"You weren't on your parents' health insurance?"

"He had better insurance. Anyway, we enjoyed being married, so here we are. Now, I'm a social worker and Alex works for an accounting firm. True love!" Gelly fluttered her lashes at Alex.

"Quite the love story," Alex quipped. Gelly reached over and punched his shoulder.

"You adore me, face it." She leaned over and smacked him on the lips.

"Ugh, not this again, Gelly," I said, holding my hands up to block the view. "You know I'm uncomfortable with PDA."

"Only because you are a sad and lonely man," and Gelly's eyes moved to Shell as she lifted her brows.

"And on that note, I think I will head to bed." Shell got up. As she turned to head inside she looked back, "thank you all," she had to clear her throat, "for everything you've done for the Heberts. There's a special place in heaven for angels like you!"

Gelly smiled and turned to me. "I like her. You should definitely make your move on this one."

"Put a little Kaluha in the hot chocolate tonight, Gelly?"

"Yes, but that doesn't negate that she," she pointed to the doorway Shell just vacated, "is a peach."

"And cute," Alex said, but when Gelly glared at him, he stammered, "Not that I'm looking, I mean, for Beau."

"I don't know how to respond except to say that Michelle is my boss. Now, I'm headed out for the first watch. Alex, I'll wake you up for the second watch, probably between midnight and two am. Then you will need to wake Etienne to take the last shift. Work for you?"

"That works. I'll head to bed so I can get some rest before my shift." He grabbed Gelly by the hand and she giggled as she followed him into the house. I didn't think that Alex intended to go right to sleep.

14

Safe and Sound

Michelle

That night I laid in bed staring at the ceiling. Although my body needed rest, I was nervous after the events of the day. As I lay there listening to the evening thunder storms roll in, I imagined Beau, stuck in the rain guarding me and my students. Eventually, I gave up, turned the bedside lamp on, and pulled out my romance novel. Time to escape reality. About an hour later, I smiled at the light knock on my door. "Yes?"

"Madame Michelle?"

"Bailey Marie?"

"*J'ai peur.*" [I'm afraid]

"*Viens ici.*" [come here] Bailey Marie climbed into bed, and I hugged her tight. After about 15 minutes, Bailey Marie's breathing had just gotten regular, indicating she was asleep, when another knock sounded.

"*Oui?*" [Yes?]

"Madame LeBlanc?" Tanner poked his head in the doorway.

"Other side," I said, and Tanner climbed in as well. A half an hour later, Valerie knocked.

"Madame LeBlanc?"

"They're both here. Come join us." All piled up on the bed, I finally fell asleep because I was watching over the Herberts while Beau was watching over us.

The next morning, I overheard Gelly and Alex talking in the living room. Probably trying to wake the Heberts, or Littles as Beau called them, for school. They were not in their beds, so I figured she would panic. To avert her panic, I reached for my phone and texted,

> The Heberts are safe here with me.

Based on the next panicky sounds outside my door, she was not checking her messages. Gelly knocked frantically on Beau's door.

"They're missing, Beau!" she yelled.

As he scrambled around his room, knocking over what I can only assume were lamps, I tried to text Beau.

> I've got them all in my room. They're sleeping.

Beau's morning voice was scratchy and disoriented. "What do you mean they are missing?!"

Finally, I tried a group text then.

> The Heberts are in my room! Stop making all that racket! They're sleeping!

These people needed to check their messages! It was to no avail. The chaos continued.

"When I tried to wake the kids, they were not in their beds." I could hear Beau stomping out of his room.

"Wait, Beau!" Gelly said.

"Wait, why? If they are missing, we have to find them now."

"First, put on some pants, or PJs, or anything else besides just your boxers. There are kids in the house, Beau ... or at least there are supposed to be."

Beau growled at his sister. I smirked, kinda wishing I could have seen him in his boxers. They moved to the kitchen. Somebody was fixing coffee. The pour and the clink of the pot made my mouth water.

"Where are they?!" Gelly yelled.

"Who?" Etienne asked.

Beau said, "The Littles. Gelly says they aren't in their beds. Are they outside?"

"No one came to or left this house. That I can promise; I would have seen them, and I just came in."

"Check the other rooms." They started flinging doors open, and when they got to my room, I was calmly reading my Kindle in bed with the Heberts sleeping soundly tucked in next to me.

"Shhhh..." I hushed them and then whispered. "Next time, check your messages." I shook my phone at them. Angelle put her hand on her heart, and Beau just took a deep breath. He worded and made a gesture for "Coffee?" I grinned and worded back, "Yes, please." They eased out of the doorway. As they exited, Gelly and Alex checked their phones and laughed when they read my messages. Beau went to make my coffee. I hoped he remembered I like it very sweet and very creamy.

I guessed he had when Gelly teased him. "So, you know how she likes her coffee, do you?"

"Don't give me that look. I've been working at the school for over three weeks. I've seen her get coffee frequently."

"So have I, but I don't remember how she likes it," Etienne teased.

"I've seen her get it more often than you."

"Nope, I just wasn't paying attention. Twenty bucks says you remembered from the first time she got coffee how she drinks it."

"I'm leaving now." He walked back to my room and carefully handed me the cup, making sure not to wake or spill coffee on the Heberts. As he exited, he cast one last look at me, sleep rumpled with my crazy hair and no make-up. He muttered, "Doug-ass, can't believe he let this woman go." Delighted, I returned to my book and sipped my perfect coffee.

Later, carefully extricating myself out from the pile of sleeping Heberts, I headed to the kitchen with my empty coffee cup. Alex was grilling bacon, eggs, and pancakes while Gelly tossed a fruit salad. Etienne was chilling on the couch with a cup of coffee and his phone.

"So, what are y'all doing this weekend?" I asked the room at large.

"Well, we had an overnight date planned and reserved at L'Auberge casino, but we will stay and hang with the Littles," Alex said.

Gelly elbowed him. "No big deal. This is more important."

"As foster parents, can you let other people babysit the kids?" I asked.

"We can leave them with a responsible adult for up to 24 hours without permission." Alex pleaded with his eyes, wanting this time away with his wife.

Hand on my chest, I reminded them, "I'm a responsible adult. One that has known the Heberts for years. I have also already been background checked."

"And I'm off duty for the weekend. We could both babysit them," Etienne offered. Gelly rubbed her forehead, considering the matter.

Alex pleaded. "C'mon Gelly, we could leave after breakfast today and be back before breakfast on Sunday to take them to church."

Gelly hedged, wavering, "I don't know."

Beau came in from the porch to see me filling my coffee cup. "I was going to get you a refill."

"Aww, that's sweet, but I needed to get up. The Littles barely noticed me leaving the bed."

"What don't you know, Gelly?" he asked.

"Alex and I, before this all began, had reservations at L'Auberge casino for a night out. We were planning on canceling this morning, but Michelle and Etienne say they can babysit the Heberts."

Beau glowered at Etienne, who just smirked back. "I'll stay here as well," Beau said.

I reasoned with Gelly. "Valerie asked that we stay all weekend, so I have clothes for two days and the first day of school. I think we were all planning to stay all weekend, so I think you should both go. We don't need five adults to safeguard three children."

Alex squeezed Gelly's hand. "C'mon, Gelly, please! You are always working, leaving early and staying late … we need this time together."

Piling it on, I added, "It really is no problem, Gelly, and I'm an educator who has known the Hebert's for four years. It's clear they are comfortable with me, and I have a deputy and a soldier to protect us."

"Marine," Gelly and Beau both said in unison.

"My mistake, a Marine."

"Which, as everyone knows, is even better than a soldier," Beau smirked at Etienne, "or a sailor."

"Hardly!" Etienne scoffed. But since they were getting their way, he did not pursue the argument.

Gelly relented. "Fine!"

"Woo-hoo!" Alex grabbed her and did a zydeco two-step, side together, back together, and swung her around the room.

Valerie came in, rubbing her eyes. "What's going on?"

Kneeling in front of her, I brushed her hair from her eyes. "What's going on is you, Tanner, Bailey-Maire and I get to go glamping with M. Beau and M. Etienne all weekend long, while Ms. Gelly and Mr. Alex do boring adult stuff."

Valerie perked up. "Glamping?"

"It is like camping, but with running water," Beau said.

Valerie's eyes opened wide. "Like the girl scouts and boy scouts?"

"Yes." I grinned.

She grinned back. "Can we even get badges?"

"Uhh." Thinking of my mom's sewing skills, I said, "Yes, yes you can. So, what we need you to do after breakfast is sit with Tanner and Bailey Marie and tell us which skills you want to learn. I will supervise and M. Beau and M. Etienne will teach you whatever y'all want to learn, within reason." Valerie zoomed out of the room to wake up and tell her siblings.

"Sneaky way to get them to breakfast," Alex said and finished plating our food.

"I have my ways." Cue Cheshire Cat grin.

15

Smatte [Smart]

Beau

Breakfast was a raucous occasion, with the Heberts discussing and debating which skills they needed to learn.

"How many skills do you think you can teach us, M. Beau?" Tanner said, meeting his eyes, man to man.

"Uhhh." I had no clue.

"Well," Shell rescued me, "let's figure this out. It takes a half hour to introduce a skill, an hour to practice with help, and a half hour to show us you mastered the skill. Which is how much time, Valerie?"

"Two hours," she said and then bit into her egg.

"Correct. Two hours per skill. Tanner, how many hours are in a day?"

He took a sip of orange juice and paused to say, "Vingt-quatre, Twenty-four."

"Excellent, there are vingt-quatre, hours in a day. Now Bailey Marie, how many days in a weekend?"

"*Deux, Samedi et Dimanche.*" [two, Saturday and Sunday] Bailey Marie hadn't touched her food yet. She was busy cutting it up and putting each different food in separate piles on her plate.

"*Et en français, fantastique!* [and in French, fantastic] So what do we know so far about our problem, Valerie?"

Valerie finished chewing. "There are two days, there are twenty-four hours in each day, and each skill is going to take two hours to learn." My and Etienne's eyes grew wide.

"*Fantastique* math, Valerie. Madame George would be very proud of you. But you forgot a few variables."

Bailey Marie and Tanner looked confused, but Valerie smirked, because she knew something they didn't. "Variables are things that change what happens," she explained.

"Exactly, so the variables you left off were eating, sleeping, and relaxing, because to learn something, you also need time to relax. Teachers call that incubating," Shell explained, sipping her coffee.

"Like what you do to eggs?" Tanner asked. "We incubated an egg in class last year."

"Absolutely. Ideas, like birds, need time to grow and develop in our brains." Shell tapped her finger on her temple.

"How much time?" Valerie asked skeptically, seeing her twenty-four hours for skills being wheedled down with other useless variables.

"So about an hour to eat, and we eat three meals a day, so in two days that's…"

"Six hours," Tanner exclaimed. He and I both considered food to be of utmost importance.

Shell continued, "And how much time are you supposed to sleep? Bailey?"

"Mama says we need to sleep eight hours a day."

"That is correct, Bailey Marie. *T'es si smatte!*" [You're so smart] Bailey preened. Etienne and I were just gawking in astonishment. But Shell just continued with her impromptu lesson as we sipped another cup of coffee. Fascinated.

"Tanner, can you add that double, 8+8 for the two nights of sleep?"

"Fourteen no sixteen." He grinned and took another bite of bacon.

"So with six hours for eating and sixteen hours for sleep, what is the total?"

Still chewing his bacon, Tanner calculated aloud. "I don't know six plus sixteen, but I do know that the six plus six is twelve. Then I just add the ten from sixteen to make twenty-two."

Shell nodded. "Which variable is missing?"

Bailey Marie's hand shot up, and Shell nodded to her. "The egg one."

"Eggs-actly!" The Heberts laughed, while the rest of us rolled our eyes. Apparently, non-teaching adults don't understand kid humor.

"Incubation one hour per skill. So if the skills take two hours each and we add incubation for each skill, that is—"

"—Three!!!" Bailey showed two fingers on one hand and one on the other.

"Bailey Marie, you can already add in kindergarten. Wow!" She leaned over and gave her a high five across the table.

"So Valerie, let's put it all together. We have forty-eight hours, twenty-two of which are spent on other variables."

Valerie ran to her backpack and got out a math notepad with the grid paper and a pencil. She lined up the problem in the squares and solved it. She raised her head and smiled.

"That is twenty-six hours for skills!"

"Fantastique! *N'oublie pas.* [Don't forget] We need three hours per skill."

"I'm going to have to divide, aren't I?" Valerie pouted.

"You are indeed." Shell nodded with a grin.

Valerie sighed. Apparently not yet a fan of division. She turned to a new page in her notebook and worked out the problem. "Twenty-six divided by three is eight, with a remainder of two."

"So eight skills in two days. What do you want to do with the remaining two hours?"

"Recess!" they said in unison.

"Recess it is! So now you have it. You have four skills a day to select, eight skills total. Why don't you each come up with four things you want to learn? After which we'll narrow it down to the ones that will be the easiest to do this weekend." Shell pulled out a pen with three colors from her purse and handed it to Valerie.

"Each of you choose a color, so we're sure everyone had a turn in deciding." The Littles ran to their room and began working on their list.

We just stared at Shell. I asked, "What was that? It's like you taught them math and science and cooperation in like five minutes at three different levels."

"I did," Shell preened. "What can I say? Teaching is my love language. That's why I run a school. This was easy. Normally I have to do it all in French. Well, I need to call my mama to make sure she can make those badges." With that, she took her coffee cup and grabbed her cell phone and walked to the porch.

Etienne and I spent the next two days teaching the Littles the skills that they wanted to learn. Setting lures, making a camp, starting and cooking over fire, and finding your way with and without a compass. The obvious survival skills were in Valerie's handwriting.

"I don't think she trusts us to take care of her," Shell groused.

"Don't worry Shell, it is just a backup plan. You always have those as well." I used her nickname to cheer her up.

Tanner just wanted to learn how to track and use a slingshot. Bailey Marie wanted to learn how to make biscuits and do braids. Tanner balked at the hair braiding.

"Don't worry, Sport, I can teach you how to tie knots while they braid," Etienne said. The girls squinted and glared at him, highlighting his misstep.

"We'll call it a braiding and knotting workshop and you can choose what you want to learn. Sound good?" Shell was skilled at diffusing angry students.

The badge training was a hit. The Littles learned, practiced, and then demonstrated their skills with Etienne and me. While Shell coordinated with her mom, Ms. Ellie Mae, to design and sew the badges they earned.

When we had finished on Sunday, Shell's parents pulled up outside the camp.

"I hear we have some really skilled students here." Ms. Ellie Mae beamed. "Hi, I'm Madame Michelle's mama, Ms. Ellie Mae, and this is Mr. Bruce. We heard that you all learned some amazing skills this weekend. Question? Who likes Jambalaya?" All the Little's hands shot up, as did mine and Etienne's. Shell laughed and raised her hand. Mr. Bruce lifted the big Magnalite pot out of the backseat and proceeded into the camp. Ms. Ellie Mae followed with two gallons of Raising Cane sweet tea and a bag of toast. The Heberts followed the LeBlancs and their food in. Etienne and I were not far behind. Ms. Ellie Mae called out the door.

"Shell, get that package for me, will you?"

Shell reached into the car and pull out a big paper bag. She peeked inside, grinned, and said, "Perfect." Then she headed in with her loot.

After a supper of jambalaya, bread, sweet tea, and homemade cookies, the Littles were bouncing off the walls. Shell sent them out to play. She made sure Etienne watched over them while

Mr. Bruce drank coffee, supervising from his rocking chair on the porch.

"These are perfect! Thanks, Mama." Shell laid out her treasures on the bed.

"I always know I've done well when you call me Mama and not that grown up Mom or even worse Mother."

"I didn't know you had a preference. Look at this stitchwork! Perfect!"

Ms. Ellie Mae beamed. "I'm thrilled you like them."

I peered over Shell's shoulder for a closer look. Not only had Ms. Ellie Mae created badges, but she had sewn them onto the sleeves of school jackets. The jackets were the ones that the school sold to raise money. Normally displayed in the school reception area, the teachers told me that the school often gave jackets as gifts (particularly to students without warm jackets). Sipping tea, I reflected on the shared traits of kindness and giving between mother and daughter. Shell's beaming smile tugged at my own lips, causing me to forget momentarily that she was my boss. The lines between us were blurring.

The Littles came back in at sunset. Shell and Ms. Ellie Mae stood grinning outside the Little's bedroom door.

"So, because of all your hard work and to remind you of how much you learned. Ms. Ellie Mae has a surprise for you."

"It was Madame Michelle's idea," Ms. Ellie Mae said, knowing that was what the kids call her. The children edged into the rooms, not knowing what to expect. When they got inside, they marveled at the three school bomber jackets displayed on the bed. Etienne and I watched from the doorway. On the sleeves of the bomber jackets, French badges indicated which skills the Littles had learned.

Shell kneeled to speak to them. "I wanted to thank you three. Y'all gave me a 'bunny day' for a school summer camp where we work on skills to get everyone badges."

"Pretty and pink!" Bailey Marie grabbed her jacket and immediately put it on.

"Black and Gold, like the Saints!" Tanner danced around the room, hugging his new jacket.

"How did you find a periwinkle jacket? That's my favorite color!" Tears shimmered in Valerie's eyes. They wasted no time in donning their jackets.

Shell beamed. "Do you like them?"

"They're perfect! Tanner, Bailey Marie, what do you say?" Valerie prodded them.

Tanner looked very serious when he turned to Etienne and me and said, "Thank you for teaching us the skills, and thank you for our new jackets. Mine is *parfait*." [perfect]

"Mine too! *Merci, merci!*" Bailey Marie beamed.

Valerie just went up to Shell and hugged her. "I knew the school would take care of us. Thank you for being there for us. I was so scared. I feel safer." Shell hugged her tighter. When Valerie turned and hugged me as well, I vowed to myself then and there to always protect the Heberts.

16

First Day of School

Michelle

Camp Babineaux was buzzing as the sun rose on our first day of school. Although I woke up at four am, I stayed in bed planning and writing my lists. Through my open door, I saw Beau already up and making coffee. Bless him! He and Etienne had kept guard that night. After the children went to bed, I received a series of mysterious hang up calls, leaving us feeling uneasy and prompting Etienne and Beau to resume guard duty.

"Coffee?" Beau asked and delivered my perfect coffee to me in bed. Such a luxury! I beamed up at him.

"Morning, and thank you! This is perfect."

"So, do you have your checklists for the day?" he asked. He knew by now that I lived by my checklists.

"Nearly all done. Mmm, this is perfect." After organizing my raft of lists and drinking near to a gallon of coffee, I got dressed and headed to school. I made sure that Gelly was awake. She and Alex had arrived late on Sunday. They were planning to bring the children early, but not "Madame Michelle early," as Gelly said. Once I verified they had the Littles in hand, I grabbed my keys and made for the door.

Beau caught up with me before I even got to the porch. "Let's head out together."

I shook my head. "Too early. Relax and have some coffee."

Beau shook his head back and whispered in case the Littles were awake. "Nope. Doug-ass is still out there. He has twice tried to strong-arm you when he thought you were alone. I too have a list of tasks to complete today, so I'm coming with you."

"Fine, but hurry."

Beau glanced at his watch. "It is five am and school starts at eight am. Why are you getting there so early?"

"First day of school!" I said with a goofy grin on my face.

Beau rolled his eyes and shook his head. "Teachers."

"I know, aren't we awesome?! Onward!" I stage whispered, and I charged to my car.

In Teacherland, this first day of school went off without a hitch ... for the most part. One parent came in mad that the students shared supplies, calling the practice communism. But I explained the supplies were for the teacher, not the students. To prevent teachers from using personal funds for student supplies. I let her know the students were welcome to bring a school box with their own private supplies. However, the teacher might send them home if those supplies interfered with learning because students were fighting, stealing, or gloating over them.

A few students came to school without uniforms. Teachers simply sent them to the pantry to pick out a free uniform, to avoid losing too much instructional time. I hired two of our regular substitute teachers and paid them a full day so I could put them wherever I needed them whenever I needed them that day. I had them take all duty hours, so that teachers got enough breaks to handle the additional administration required on day one.

Beau just tried to keep up. He was cleaning spills, cleaning bathroom accidents, picking up trash, and even helping with coffee runs. Needing to keep my teachers caffeinated, I created a system where they buzzed in to the office when they needed more coffee. It took loads of energy to teach. Beau's primary task, however, was to oversee installing the new security system. The board had refused to pay for it, so I decided to pay for it myself. This led to our first argument.

"Just ask your friend Marc to send me the bill," I said.

As Beau shook his head, his curls bounced. "I know the board isn't paying for it, Shell, and I'm not letting you pay for it."

Even my patented annoyed glare, with hands on my hips, and the statement, "My school, my costs," did not work with *tête dure* Beau Babineaux.

"Not this time. I told you my dad invested all that money for me. I can take a little out and gift it to the school. It's for my own peace of mind. Besides, Marc will give me a bargain basement deal. Also, he wants to know if you have a place in kindergarten for another student. My goddaughter Sofia is five, and he wants her to learn French." Beau had mastered the skill of distracting me.

"Kindergarten, yes, we still have three places left. Give me Marc's phone number, and I'll call him to bring Sofia by today." Beau gave me the number and then walked off, smirking. I yelled at him through my office door. "I only relented because I'm taking everyone out tonight to reward them for a successful first day."

"Whatever it takes," he yelled back and then walked off whistling.

At the end of the day, I got on the intercom, "Choir practice at Little Big Cup on me. Nice first day everyone," and then translated that into French.

Beau knocked on my office door and peaked in. "Choir practice, huh? I've heard about that."

"From whom? It is a teacher's secret."

He grinned. "Renee."

"I'm going to have to speak to Renee about divulging our secrets. Let me make sure Gelly and Alex have the kids, then you want to come with me to Choir practice at Little Big Cup?"

"I can sing a few rounds. Actually, I'll have some of their Swamp Pop filé root beer to make sure there you have a designated driver. After today, I think you might need a second drink or a third."

I held up two fingers. "I'm a strict two drink limit kinda girl."

"But you're tiny, so two drinks probably puts you over the driving limit. Let me help."

I rolled my eyes thinking, *size sixteen is hardly tiny*, but since Beau was a giant, I guess size was relative.

At the Little Big Cup, the owners welcomed the group. Ever the planner, I had called ahead to reserve a table next to the Bayou Teche. I paid for four pitchers of beer, three pitchers of diet coke, and two pitchers of Zatarain root beer. Then I added several orders of crawfish cornbread, mac and cheese balls, and sweet potato fries. First day of school work makes one hungry and thirsty. Then the teachers arrived.

$$\text{17}$$

Choir Practice

Beau

That crew of teachers was a rowdy crew, and Shell welcomed them with open arms. She started with a toast.

"À la nouvelle année, [to a new year] to teaching, learning, and having un bon temps." [a good time]

The other teachers toasted with her, and "Choir Practice" began. "Choir Practice" included a variety of alcoholic and non-alcoholic libations and a table filled with delicious appetizers to share. Shell was in her element. Speaking in English to one colleague and French to another.

Despite speaking French, I struggled to understand their rapid conversation about topics outside my ken. I held my own, but unlike Shell, I could not simultaneously interpret. She was pretty damn impressive. Most impressive was when the bill came, she paid for everything. The teachers complained, but to no avail.

"This is a reward for all the hard work you've already done and all the hard work you will be doing. Plus, at some point in the year, I'm gonna ask you to do something that you either won't want or have the energy to do. This is me paying it forward before that time comes." So they relented and thanked her graciously. Then she added, "Plus, Beau paid for the security system that I had already budgeted for so I had some money *lagniappe*!"

They raised their glasses to us both.

"*Santé*," they said, "*À* Beau *et à* Michelle." [Cheers to Beau and Michelle]

Besides the raised glasses, I couldn't help but notice a few raised eyebrows and knowing nods exchanged between some of the male teachers. I glared at them for their disrespect. Unsure of my intentions, they glared back at me with suspicion. They nodded, an unspoken truce, when Shell beamed up at me and brushed a curl behind her ear. By five thirty, Shell prepared to leave.

"After this, you are on your own. Remember, if you've had more than one drink, I'll pay you back for your Uber or a taxi home. No Académie teachers will be on the news for drunk driving. See you all bright and early in the morning. There will be plenty of coffee."

They raised their glasses again. "To coffee!" Several teachers left with us. Only the youngest remained. Shell chatted with the manager before she left.

"Taxis or Ubers for everyone. You know I'm good for it, and I'll pay you double."

The manager nodded. "Yes ma'am. We have it under control."

Shell was not drunk, but she was tipsy, and like my cousin Renee, she was a friendly drunk/tipsy person. Maybe it was just a teacher thing. My fingers dug into her soft waist as I lifted her into my truck. When I hopped in after loading her up, my truck cab smelled of snickerdoodles. The deep inhale I took to calm my nerves only seared that scent into my memory. *Think of something else, Marine!*

"Beau?" She leaned over, put her head on my shoulder, and gazed up at me.

"Yes." With a turn of the key in the ignition, I started up Big Betsy, and headed to her place.

"Beau, I like you," she said, still gazing up at me.

Eyes on the road, I responded, "I like you too."

"No, I like like you."

My lip twitched. "I like, like you too."

"No, you don't." She shook her head and her curls brushed my neck.

The scent of cinnamon rolls filled the truck. "Yes, yes, I do."

"Well, then, why don't you kiss me?" She pouted at that and I had to smile.

Eyes on the road, Marine. "Because you're my boss."

She shook her head again, and I smelled sugar cookies. "No, the school board is your boss. I'm your supervisor."

"Potato, potahto, patate (French version)." She sighed deeply and kept her head resting on my chest.

Since Gelly and Alex had the Littles tonight, I drove her to her garage apartment. The ride was peaceful, and she ended up falling asleep on my shoulder as we drove. It felt ... nice. It felt ... right. When we arrived at her apartment, I leaned my head against hers and took in one last whiff of her scent. Gooey cinnamon rolls. She was a walking dessert.

"We're here." She lifted her head and looked at me. My gaze trapped in hers. But she was my boss no matter what she said. To break the moment I asked, "Why don't you live someplace nicer?" She gave me a Mona Lisa smile.

"If I live someplace nicer, who would pick up the tab for the teachers? Who would stock the school pantry or buy the extra uniforms? This is perfect for me. What's important, Beau is making a difference and not material possessions. I want to make a difference." With that, she leaned over, sloppily kissed me on the cheek, and tried to exit the truck.

She tugged at the door. "It's locked."

"Yes, you fell last time when you were stone cold sober. Tonight, I'm helping you get down."

Rounding the truck, I opened the door and grabbed Shell by her waist, gently lowering her to the ground.

"That was nice. Can we do it again?" Delighted, I lifted her back up and lowered her again. "You're very good at that."

"Thank you." Then I walked her up the steps. She turned around in her doorway and gazed blearily up at me. "My car is at the Little Big Cup."

My mouth twitched. "I'll pick you up tomorrow morning."

"I'll have coffee."

"Sounds good. Goodnight Shell."

"*Bonne nuit*, Beau." She closed the door, and then called out, "I still think you should kiss me."

With a stupid grin, I jogged down the stairs, hopped in my truck, and headed back to the camp for sentry duty.

Michelle

The next three weeks fell into a routine. Beau and I had coffee every morning on my tiny porch before heading to the camp. Once at camp, we poured another cup of coffee and 'porch sat' while waiting for the Littles. Each day Gelly and Alex woke them up and dressed them, then we walked them through the woods to the cafeteria for breakfast. After school, we'd often eat together at camp with Gelly and Alex and the Littles, with colleagues, and occasionally with just the two of us.

On the weekends, Beau, Etienne, and I would relieve Gelly and Alex and have badge earning sessions. The Heberts were transforming into homesteaders. They even got several chickens, and Beau taught them how to feed them and collect eggs. They learned basic carpentry and even fun codes, such as Morse and basic ASL.

By the second weekend, I ended up joining them. What can I say? I love to learn. Plus, I wanted to earn all the cool badges as well. Mama even made me my own bomber jacket on which to sew the badges. She even invited the Krewe to her house to learn important gardening skills.

"Shell, you're a mystery. For years, you rejected my attempts to try to teach you canning, pickling, and how to dry food. Now you can't learn enough!" Mama said as we worked together in the garden.

"Couldn't say. It's just more interesting through the eyes of children. Plus, you never once gave me a badge." I grinned.

One of Mama's eyebrows lifted. "I'm sure it has nothing to do with the handsome *concierge* that is teaching the skills?"

"Nope, of course not. I'm sure I don't know what you're talking about." I started meticulously planting each vegetable as diagrammed on the chart Beau had made me ... us.

"Young lady, you live on our property. You think we haven't noticed that your Beau comes over every morning for coffee?"

"We have a lot to discuss." My gaze stayed focused on the plants and the garden design. Mama could read me like a book.

"Uh, huh? If you are telling me it is all work related, then I'll have to call you a liar."

Exasperated, I turned to her. "I like him, but I'm also his boss and I can't risk things going wrong. I have my school to consider."

"He's courting you," my mama said.

"No, we are just taking care of the Littles together."

She whispered in my ear. "I like him."

"Me too, Mama, but it can't happen. He is just being kind."

She snorted at that. "If that were true, he would just do activities with the Littles. His Mama believes he's smitten."

"Not now, Mama. I have things to do and a school to run."

"Madame LeBlanc?" *Saved by the Val.* I bit my lip. "Can you tell me which one of these is chard and which is kale? They look so alike."

I gave her a side hug and brushed her bangs out of her eyes. "That is because they originally were the same plant, but they bred them to have specific qualities."

As Beau continued to run what I considered to be our 'homesteading workshops', I kept forgetting I was his boss ... supervisor. I needed to focus on learning the skills and not get sidetracked.

"Looking good! Will you be able to can all of those veggies?" Beau asked me over my shoulder. His breath was a warm wind on my ear, but I ignored it, because I'm a consummate professional. *Deflect, deflect,* my brain warned.

"Are you kidding me? I'm getting to be so skilled that I'm going to be called in at any moment to help the Raneys on 'Homestead Rescue'."

He cocked his head to the side? "Is that another cultural reference?"

"Remind me we need to add a pop culture hangout night to our agenda. You have twenty years to catch up on."

"It's a date." He smiled, and then I just blinked, imagining what I truly wanted to happen on our date. Beau raised his brows.

The next week, we were at the Babineaux farm. While Beau told me many parental unit stories, I hadn't met Ms. Denise and Mr. Herman in person. Apparently, my mama was in close contact with them. Mr. Herman joined in on the fun, teaching me and the Littles how to saddle, ride, and brush a horse and even clean out stalls.

Tanner and Bailey Marie were in heaven. Apparently, they were horse fiends from way back. Valerie was more circumspect. "It smells funny in here," she said and sidled up next to Beau. He made her feel safe. Me too. Closing my eyes, I contemplated what that meant. When I opened them, he was right there.

"Whatcha thinking about?" He whispered in my ear. His hot breath on my ear was not helping.

I turned to watch the Littles. "What do you mean?"

"You blink and close your eyes for no reason, and I'm thinking that you're thinking about things that I need to know."

"No." After a shake of my head, I turned away from him.

More hot breath in my ear. "No, you aren't thinking about things, or, no, I can't know what you're thinking."

"The second one."

"That's what I thought." He smirked and walked off. I turned around and noted Mr. Herman wearing an identical smirk.

"Can I help you with anything, Mr. Herman?"

"No, I'm good. Why don't you help my wife set up lunch?" He tilted his head toward the main house, as they called it. A big Acadian house with an enormous front porch, on which Ms. Denise and my very own mama were setting up for a late outdoor luncheon.

We ate a scrumptious lunch of pulled pork sandwiches and watermelon slices on their big front porch. As we ate, I thought, *maybe I'm ready to move out of my parent's apartment. With all my new homesteading skills, I should move to a farm.*

Beau whispered in my ear. "I don't know if I would say you have all the skills, Shell. But even if I sometimes gripe, farm life is the good life."

"Oh God, did I say that out loud?!" My face turned sunburned red.

"That you did Shell, that you did." And with that began the thoughts, the ones I was supposed to avoid assiduously. I blinked them away. Beau's smile met me when I opened my eyes and I grinned back. *Oh oh, I might be in trouble.*

18

Les flammes d'enfer [The Fires of Hell]

Beau

Sitting in a booth at Just Judy's, a country biker bar, was a challenge. Everyone in the Krewe felt uneasy facing away from the door, but it wasn't feasible for all four of us to sit on one side. Compromising, we took turns. Tonight it was Etienne and my turns. My back was itching, and Etienne did not look comfortable either. Maybe our libations would help ease the stress.

"Don't look now, but I think that Doug-ass person just walked in." Marc told us, and Etienne and I both stiffened. He had been keeping his distance, but men who assaulted their ex-wives were not to be trusted.

"What's he doing?" I asked.

"Scanning, searching for a spot, I would say. He is looking this way. Don't turn," Armand said, "Annnnd … he's heading this way."

Doug sat in the booth behind us and called to the bartender. "Four shots, whatever is cheapest!" The bartender came over with a bottle and four shot glasses.

"Just leave the bottle," he slurred. Somebody drank before he went out drinking. His stench wafted towards the booth. With a wave of my phone, I indicated it was time for a text conversation.

> Etienne: Smells like someone is on a bender. (skunk emoji)

"Keys first," the bartender said.

"Fuck you, I'm fine," Doug responded.

The bartender did not relent. "Keys or no booze."

"Fine, here, and fuck off."

"Whatever," the barkeep said and then nodded to our table. Marc shook his head at him, so he did not come to our table. We were in full reconnaissance mode.

> What's he doing?

> Marc: Checking his phone

"Fucking Cubs! God damn Pelicans! Two grand, fucking lost me, two grand!"

> Marc: Oh, oh! Methinks someone is sports gambling (crazy face emoji)

Doug's phone vibrated. He did not answer, but it kept vibrating. He finally gave up and answered. At cringe decibel, we heard from the other end of the line, "Where's my fucking money?!"

Doug responded, "I don't know what you are talking about, Stephie."

Etienne: Stephie?

New wife

Then her voice got muffled and we could only make out "*Sports gambling! What the fuck, Doug?*" We couldn't hear the rest, but we could extrapolate. Doug was screwed.

"Chill Stephie, just use the credit cards." More muffled sounds, another yell of "*Sports gambling!*" Doug pled, "Stephie, I'm in a funk because I lost another job." From there, we could only hear Doug's end of the conversation. "Don't worry. My dad will give me a loan. It will be fine. Once I sell the land Pops gave me, we'll be in the clear."

Land that was being leased to Académie School. Etienne, and my eyes met. Etienne pulled out his ever-present notebook and wrote, 'sports gambling'. They ended the conversation with Stephie, yelling, "I'm done!"

Marc: Smart Stephie

We all smiled. Doug slammed down two more shots and then dialed his phone. We listened to his side of the conversation.

"Dad, hey how's it going? Not good. Stephie left, and I lost my job. Listen, can you loan me more money? ... Right, right, the South street apartments. I have it under control. Just need an advance on my paycheck?... Yeah. No problems. Just a few welfare queens that don't want to pay their bills. So entitled. They need to get jobs and stop suckling off Uncle Sam's tit. Our lawyer he wrote up the eviction letters for me ... No, I didn't know that you can request to see if and who cashed your check."

Then his dad screaming on the phone. "*You dumbass ...
lawsuits ... forgery ... steal from me ... we are done!*" Etienne
added 'forgery,' to his notebook.

Doug-ass is toast. What's he doing now?

Marc: He took a shot for courage & now
he's dialing.

Armand: Probably, mommy, LOL!

Doug cursed again, then his phone vibrated. He said, "Shit,
shit, shit" and answered immediately. This was an enlightening
conversation.

"No, Mr. Breaux, I'm still working on it."

"*I want that land,*" was all we discerned from the other end of
the conversation. Etienne jotted down, 'Mr. Breaux and Land'.

"I told you I'm working on it. My lawyers said they can't
break the lease and I can't get my bitch of an ex-wife to get off
the property. No! I need my house and my car. I need more time
to get you your casino land ... Okay, within the month, you'll
have your lease."

Etienne added 'casino' to his notebook.

"I need more time than that. Fine. A week." He hung up.
Armand signaled for another round as Doug downed a couple
more shots. We had just gotten our next drink when he made
the most interesting call. "I need help! You owe me, Ray!"

Etienne quickly added, 'Ray? Same Ray?' to his notebook.

Doug downed another shot. "The boss wants it done within
the week ... I can't talk here. Where can we meet?... That's in
the middle of bum fuck Egypt! No, you pick me up where we
usually meet. The bartender has my keys, and I need to do this
now ... Whatever, when?" after the mysterious Ray responded,

Doug signed off with, "I'll see you then." He took a last shot, threw money on the table, and left.

Urgently, Etienne dialed his office and requested to speak to the on-duty deputy.

"The Ultron Ray that we are looking for, see if you can find any Rays that meet his description with known associates with the last name Breaux. Also, we need a cruiser to swing by the Académie Immersion School. I just overheard a credible threat."

Etienne turned to us. "I'm going to follow him. Where is Michelle now?"

"With Gelly and the Littles at the camp," I said.

"Alone!?" Armand asked.

"Of course not, Alex is there."

Etienne headed to the door. "I'd feel better if y'all headed over there. My cousin is the best, but he is not much of a brawler, and it sounds like something is going down."

Michelle

"How did we lose sight of them!" Gelly said.

"Sorry. I just turned around for a second, and they were gone," Alex said, rubbing his forehead. "I'm not good at this Gelly!"

"It's okay sweetie, we will find them," she put her hand on his shoulder and squeezed.

"I'm texting Beau." I let them know.

Kids snuck off

Beau: On my way,

Ten minutes later, the Heberts came running out of the woods with three dogs trailing after them. Torn between wanting to hug them and scold them, I opted for the former. I chose to wait for their explanation. "Why, why, why did you run off?" I took a deep breath. They were fine. No time to panic.

Tanner tugged on my arm. "We saw that bad guy."

I kneeled down to listen to him. "Which bad guy?"

Val answered for them. "Mr. Blake, the one that grabbed you. He was going to grab us, but the dogs chased him away. I think he is coming after us!"

In an instant, I whipped out my phone and called Etienne. "Etienne, the kids spotted Doug in the woods. I thought there was a restraining order on him."

"There is. I'll call it in. I'm on my way there. Are Marc, Armand, and Beau there, yet?"

"Beau is on his way. I don't know about the others."

"They are with him. Get inside the camp. Have Alex stand guard and wait for Beau and the Krewe."

I got off the phone with Etienne. Alex ushered us into the camp, double-checking that we locked the door. The three dogs that had followed the Littles to camp were outside and growling. Something or someone was coming. Beau texted to the group.

Beau: Nearly there. Etienne, get a car out there!

But it was too late. I watched through the window. As Alex was reading the message, Doug snuck up behind him and cracked his skull with a baseball bat. He swung at the dogs as well. They gave him some space, but were growling ferociously. He shot at them and they ran to the back. Freed from the dogs, Doug grabbed a gasoline can from behind a tree and poured it around the house. I called Beau in a panic. "Beau, Doug just clobbered Alex. I repeat, Alex is down. Get an ambulance. Doug's pouring gasoline around the house, and he has a gun!"

"He's trying to smoke you out, Shell. Do not go outside unless you have to. Doug will probably be waiting with his gun at the front door." I tried to sneak a peek out the window and Doug fired into the house, smashing the window.

"Big Bedroom," Gelly said and ushered the Littles and me into the room with the attached bathroom. Each child placed a wet towel on themselves, then the remaining towels were used to block the door seams. Another shot shattered the back window as Gelly looked out. The stray dogs' growls grew louder.

"He has someone with him, shots in the front and the back," I warned them. Gelly and I made the Littles lay over spaces in the floorboards so they could breathe. While we were out of towels, we scrounged up a few old t-shirts, wet them and wrapped them around our heads and bodies. Sirens screamed outside, a barrage of gunfire sounded, and those dogs, bless them, were barking and chasing after someone. Then Beau was at the window.

"Get out, get out, get out!" he yelled. Gelly and I handed the Littles out through the window. I, closer to the window, climbed through.

"Gelly!" Beau yelled. I turned just as a rafter fell, pinning Gelly in place. Beau jumped into the house the instant the burning rafter hit Gelly. He used another board to lever the rafter off of her and carried her out the window. The rafter injured her face and the right side of her body.

"Alex!" Gelly cried.

"I'll find him, I'll make sure he is in an ambulance," Beau told her as EMTs loaded her into an ambulance.

"Doug hit him really hard, like really hard. He was right outside the side porch," she said as an EMT put her in an ambulance. I was with the Littles with another EMT getting them checked out.

Etienne and Beau wasted no time in finding Alex.

"Here! We need a medic here!" Etienne cried when he discovered Alex's crumpled form. Beau searched for a pulse. He nodded, but did not look hopeful.

"Still alive, thank God!" he said.

"EMTs!!! Over here now!" Etienne yelled. The EMTs arrived and loaded Alex into the ambulance.

I huddled under a tree, hugging the Littles to me. They gripped me tightly, their faces ashen and their chins trembling. Etienne and Beau walked toward us.

"It was the bad man!" Valerie yelled, pointing at Doug's still form.

"I know *ma cherie,* [my dear] he won't hurt us again." Beau brushed her hair out of her fact.

There was a tremor in her voice when she asked, "But what about Ms. Gelly and Mr. Alex? They are supposed to take care of us."

"You can stay with me until they get better." Wondering how they would all fit into my studio apartment, I called my parents.

"There's been a fire. The Littles foster parents were both hurt. Can I bring—?"

"Of course you can. You get here right away, and we will have beds made up for all of you." My mama's voice calmed me.

"Thanks Mama!" At this point, Beau's arm wrapped around me as he gave me a supportive side hug. I leaned against him as he spoke on the phone to his parents. He updated them on Alex's and Gelly's conditions. They were rushing to the hospital to see about Gelly and Alex.

"I'll meet you there once I get Shell and the Littles situated," he said.

I shook my head. "We can get there on our own. Go check on your sister."

"Shhh." He kissed my forehead. "The doctors are taking care of them. They probably won't be able to tell us anything for a while. Please let me make sure that you and the Littles are okay."

I nodded and moved to hug the crying children.

19

The Aftermath

Beau

When I dropped off the Littles and a bewildered Shell at her parents, Ms. Ellie Mae was a rock. She opened the door before we could knock. "Come here, my precious dears. We have a room for you to sleep in." She gave them a hug and ushered them inside.

Valerie resisted. "With Madame Michelle?" she asked.

Ms. Ellie Mae studied her daughter, who nodded. "Of course, ma chère, [my dear] with an enormous bed that you can all snuggle up in. Madame Michelle and her sisters have extra pajamas for you and Miss Bailey Marie. Tanner, Mr. Bruce has an old Saints shirt for you to sleep in." She herded the Littles toward the hallway and turned to me. "I have this in hand. You get on over to the hospital. I'm praying for your sister and brother-in-law. Shell, see him out, please."

"Oui maman," [yes mama] she said and turned to me.

"I gotta go," I said, reaching for and squeezing her hand. Shell nodded and squeezed my hand back.

"I'll call you from the hospital."

She nodded. "Text. The Littles will no doubt all snuggle with me tonight, and I won't want to wake them."

Looking forlorn, covered in soot and sweat, her hair a mass of messy curls, I stared at her. Unable to resist, I grabbed her by the waist, giving her a firm kiss that left us both momentarily breathless. "I'm so glad you're okay," I said, relieved. Her discombobulated expression brought a smile to my face. "I'll text."

As she closed the door, she said, "Thank you for rescuing us." Our eyes locked, and I thought *I couldn't imagine a world without you in it*, but I said nothing. Turning, I swiftly rushed to the hospital. En route, I called Marc.

"What a FUBAR! What's the situation at the camp?"

"Etienne is chasing after Ray. Apparently, he has a blood sample now because the dogs that chased him off all got a bite of him. So, we might have a better lead, if this is the same as Ultron Ray."

"Tell Armand to guard the LeBlanc house. Tell him to check his texts for the address. The Littles and Shell are there. Make sure they're protected. I need to check on Gelly and Alex in the hospital."

"I'm on it," Armand said in the background.

"Any other developments?" With a flick of the ignition, Big Betsy rumbled to life, and I sped out the drive.

"Well, the camp is being guarded by those three dogs that bit Ray," Marc said.

"Check if they're injured and get some steaks delivered, rare. They deserve a reward."

"If you feed them, they will stay."

"That's the plan. We need guard dogs for the Littles and they have apparently appointed themselves. I'll come pick them up tomorrow. Can you stay on watch over there tonight?"

"Already called my mom about watching Sofia," Marc said.

Exhaling, I felt a little relief. My Krewe had my back. "Thanks man!"

"Just let us know how Gelly and Alex are."

"Will do," I said, and I hung up.

When I got to the hospital, my parents were already waiting outside the emergency room. My cousin Renee and Aunt Emma were also there.

"They took them both into surgery," my mama said.

"How long ago?" I asked, knowing that the longer the surgery, the worse the injury.

She glanced at her watch. "About a half hour."

A doctor approached the desk, questioned the receptionist, and then headed towards us. "Mr. and Mrs. Babineaux?"

"Yes?" my mama said and reached for my father's hand.

"I'm Dr. Daigle, Mrs. Landry, Angelle, is stable. She had a gash from whatever fell on her."

"A rafter ... in the fire." I told him.

"Well, apparently it did not crush her, and she was immediately extricated from there, so apart from the scarring, which will be extensive, she is going to be fine. It will be a long recovery." Exhaling, I experienced a wave of relief.

"And Alex?" I asked.

"Mr. Landry is another story. He had severe trauma to the head. While he's breathing on his own, we needed to put him into a medically induced coma. We repaired what we could, but it's a wait and see game. It is a brain injury, and those are hard to predict in terms of repair. He is not brain dead, so that is positive news. That is the best I can tell you at this point."

"So, he may recover?" my mama asked.

"Yes, he may, but he may not. I don't want to give you false hope."

"When will Gelly be able to visit him?" I asked.

"Probably in a day or two. She will be in a lot of pain, but we will control it."

"The least amount you can give her," I told the doctor.

He raised his eyebrows in surprise.

"As a social worker, she works with a lot of drug addicts, or as she calls them people with overuse disorders. Believe me when I tell you, she'll want the absolute minimum, and she'll want to be weaned off of them immediately."

"Noted. Once she awakes from surgery, we'll discuss that with her and follow her preferences. You should be able to visit Mrs. Landry tomorrow morning. The nurse has your contacts. If there are any changes, we will call you. Mr. Babineaux, give me a moment, and I will see about your hands." and Dr. Daigle went and made a note in her chart. We all glanced down at my hands. My body hadn't even registered the redness or the cuts on them. Dr. Daigle came over with bandages, burn cream, and antibiotic ointment.

"It doesn't look like you need stitches, and this cream should ease any pain. Let me know if the antibiotic doesn't work, and your hands get infected. Or let your GP know. It will be less expensive. No charge, because I'm guessing you're the reason that both your sister and brother-in-law are still alive."

"Thanks," I said when he finished, never a fan of getting praise for doing what should be done. I turned to my parents. "I need to text, Shell." They looked at my wrapped hands.

"You need help?"

"No, I'll just talk to text. I'm heading over to the LeBlanc's tonight, but be forewarned, I'm inviting them to our property ... all of them. So, prepare yourselves. They will be at my place."

My mama kissed my cheek. "Beau, I love you and your protective soul, but you will not be living in sin with a school principal on our property."

"Mama!"

"No, mama. We will discuss later how they will move into the main house, *not* your house. Go make sure they are okay and thank you for saving your sister and your brother-in-law, baby!"

My mama kissed me on the other cheek and my father hugged me. My parents held on to each other as they walked away. "We are going to the chapel to pray. You need us to pray for anything else besides Gelly and Alex's health?" my Mama asked.

"That Shell will not be stubborn?" I asked.

My father chuckled. "It's not stubborn, young man, it's assertive. I'll pray that you don't stick your foot in it."

My mama smiled, walked back, and kissed my cheek again. Returning to Daddy's side, they walked hand in hand to the hospital chapel. I went outside, got in my truck, and texted Shell as best I could using talk to text.

My phone rang. To answer it, I used an uncovered finger and placed the phone on speaker while balancing it on my knee. "Sorry, I have bandages on my hands and can't text."

"Oh no, are you OK?"

"I'm fine. What I was trying to tell you was that Gelly was badly burned and will have scars, but she is stable and should recover." I put the keys in the ignition, starting up Big Betsy.

"Stable and in recovery. Wonderful. And Alex?"

"Unknown. He is alive, but they had to put him into a coma. Has severe brain damage. They don't know if he will recover."

"But he is alive."

"Yes, but we don't know for how long and if he wakes up, he may have severe brain damage. I feel like a failure." I started up Big Betsy.

"You did all you could, Beau."

Eyes shut, I took a deep breath. "If I had gotten to him faster."

"Then you might not have rescued us and Gelly. He would not have wanted that. Let's just wait and see. He may pull out of it."

I was silent. I'd seen the initial damage and did not hold out much hope.

Shell's voice pulled me back. "Do you want to come over and talk?"

"Talk?"

I noted the smile in her voice. "We'll see. Come over. The Littles are sleeping, and I'm having a nightcap. Come join me."

"On my way, Shell. Can you text Etienne about Gelly and Alex and ask him to text the rest of the Krewe? Talk to text is not my friend."

"Sure thing, now get over here and comfort me."

20

Comfort

Michelle

I considered changing out of my pajama set, but decided that I was too tired. Slipping on a robe, I raided my dad's liquor cabinet, and pulled out the Lagavulin. What we had been through merited sixteen-year-old single malt scotch. I gave the scotch glasses a thorough polish and then filled them up with two fingers of scotch, my usual limit. Then I added a *soupçon* more, because it had been a rough night. Taking extra care, I brought the two glasses out to the screened-in porch.

Arranging Beau's scotch on the table, and I sat with mine on the porch swing. I reflected on Doug; his actions seemed odd and out of proportion. Trying to kill us all just to break a lease. The lease wasn't with me; it was with the school board. While I tried to figure the why of it all, Beau's truck pulled up. As soon as he exited the truck, a wave of relief washed over me, releasing the pent-up anxiety I hadn't even realized I was carrying.

I stood as he climbed the porch steps. "Your hands!" They were all bandaged up. I know he told me, but it's different seeing it in person.

"I'm fine. Doctor said that barring infection I won't even have scars. Unlike Gelly." He closed his eyes and rubbed his forehead.

"Beau, you did all you could. You got her out of there as soon as possible." Opening the screen door for him, I gave him a bear hug.

"My mind keeps replaying alternate scenarios, trying to figure out if I could have done it differently." I hugged him tighter.

"You arrived as soon as you could. You even warned us before you arrived." Embracing Beau tightly until his body gradually relaxed, I tenderly kissed his cheek and gestured towards the rocking chairs. He sat, and I handed him a scotch, which he clutched between his two bandaged hands. I sat on the porch swing next to him with my libation. Holding the drink with both hands, he took a sip and smiled at me.

"Lagavulin?"

I adjusted my robe and sat on the swing. "I figured we earned it. So, what happened? Is Doug really dead and what about the shooter in the back?"

"Etienne and I took care of Doug. He's dead and will not be bothering anyone anymore, but the other shooter..." Beau shook his head.

"What?"

"The shooter, the one in the back, he got away."

Worried we might be targeted, I scanned the property. "The fils d'putain [son of a bitch] isn't in attack mode. He was bitten by three dogs. There was a lot of blood left behind. He's probably fighting to stay alive at this point."

"The dogs that followed the Littles out of the woods? They said that Doug had tried to grab them and the dogs defended them. I owe them each a steak."

"I already ordered them steaks. Marc is watching the camp and feeding the dogs, and that is Armand's '71 Dodge Challenger."

"It is even yellow like Gibb's!"

"Yes, so you have both Armand and the spirit of NCIS protecting you," Beau said, and patted my knee with his bandaged hand.

"Plus there is you. You neutralized them and then rescued us. There was nothing you could have done differently."

"We let our guard down."

"Alex was there. You always had some testosterone on hand." I squeezed his wrist.

Beau shook his head. "Alex is an accountant. I should have had one of my buddies there."

"Their skulls are harder than Alex's? Let it go, Beau. You did what you could. Now come over here and comfort me." He smiled then, like I hoped he would, and joined me on the porch swing.

"Comfort you?" He sat down next to me on the swing and his arm came around my back as I leaned into the crook of his shoulder.

"Absolutely. Drink some Scotch," and I brought my cup to his mouth so he could take a sip.

"Will it make me feel better?"

I sipped after him, closed my eyes, and then inhaled to experience all the flavor. Eyes closed, I admitted, "It will make you more amenable to my whims."

He whispered in my ear, "Trust me, Shell, I am amenable to your whims already."

"Good to know," I said and snuggled against him as we sat enjoying the calm.

"Help me take these bandages off," he said after a few minutes.

"What about your burns?"

"They aren't that bad, and I want to touch you. Help me out, Shell." I helped him take off the bandages, and then we leaned back on the swing and sipped our scotch. Companionable silence turned to caressing, caressing turned to necking. Then Beau rose and reached for my hand.

"C'mon Shell, let's go someplace private." I grabbed his wrist, still worried about his hands, as I followed him up the garage stairs to my apartment. I handed him my key, and he opened my door.

"We probably should say goodbye here," I told him.

"Yes," he said as the back of his hand softly caressed my hair and then he pulled me in for a brain numbing kiss.

"So," he said as he pulled away, "I'll see you tomorrow?"

"No."

"No?" Beau tilted his head and reached up to tuck a curl behind my ear. "No, I won't see you tomorrow?"

"No, don't leave."

"Well, ok then." He followed me into my apartment, closing the door behind him.

"Because we have unfinished business," I blurted out.

"We do? What unfinished business?"

And then I launched myself at him and kissed him. I kissed him desperately and deeply. I think too hard, because our teeth clinked, and his back hit the door.

"Sorry," I apologized, raising my head. Beau's hands cradled my face as he positioned me exactly where he wanted me. With a mischievous grin, he lowered his head and playfully nibbled on my lower lip, then he kissed me deeply, his tongue tangling with mine, and then he alternated and nibbled on my upper lip. I tried to keep up, but I got lost in the sensations. My head swirled as I tasted coffee and scotch.

As he kissed me, my hands drifted down to his jeans. He must not have noticed because he jumped a bit when he felt my hands on his stomach fumbling with his button ups. He tried to reach for my wandering hands.

"I've got this. Don't want you to injure yourself." As I undid each button, I nipped at his lower lip. Task completed, I skimmed my hands to below his waistband, encircling him. He was hot and fully aroused.

"I have to tell you," I said, kissing his chest through this t-shirt and making my way down his body, "It has been a long time."

"Like riding a bike," he said, and I guffawed.

"I don't know about that."

He pulled me back up. "I won't last if you do that. Let's slow this down." He gently picked me up, scanned the apartment, and carried me, carried me, like I weighed nothing, to the bedroom. He set me down on my bed and held my shoulders to keep me down. "Let me take care of you."

I was about to ask him what he meant when plunged his hands into my pyjama shorts and his fingers began stroking me. Blushing at how wet I was, I squeezed my legs together. Beau must have noticed. "It's all good. That's exactly how I want you—wet and pliant." I snorted, and he smiled, "Now just lay back and enjoy."

"You sure I'm not supposed to be doing something?" I rasped out on a moan.

"You are doing something, enjoying yourself. That is the point."

"That can't be right." But when I moved away so I could grab him and try to reciprocate, he pushed me back down and redoubled his efforts. With one finger inside me and his other hand cupping my ass, he dipped his head and bit my nipples through my thin cami. The combination of the three sensory inputs was overwhelming; I went off like a firecracker. It had been too long.

Beau leaned down and grabbed his jeans, pulling the condom from his pocket. He sheathed himself quickly, spread my languid legs apart, and then slowly penetrated me. I had been floating on a post-coital bliss, a petit mort, when he roused me again. Beau entered slowly, then pulled out almost completely before plunging in again. Over and over, until I reached a peak. My orgasm erupted again, and I nearly bucked him off the bed. As I came back down, my passage throbbing from the aftereffects, I made tiny contented mewling sounds. The sound was the last straw for Beau, and he began thrusting urgently as his own orgasm overcame him.

We both then slept like the dead. When I awoke the next morning, I surveyed my room. Beau and I had clothes scattered everywhere. I sniffed his T-shirt, smiled at the scent of Irish Spring, and put it on. The smell of coffee drew me around the corner to my little kitchenette. When I got there, I inhaled, eyes wide opened. *Holy hell*! Beau in nothing but boxers. He resembled a standing version of Rodin's thinker, sculpted perfection. I mean, I had felt how powerful he was last night. He was perfect, and I was me. And, he had not only made coffee but also *pain perdu*. [French toast]

"Do you have powdered sugar?" he started searching my cupboards.

"I don't know. Maybe. That is to say..." Beau smiled as I babbled and searched my kitchen. I was a mess.

"Right here, sugar." He held up the sugar bag from my fridge.

"Very punny."

"Are you okay?" He handed me a cup of steaming coffee made exactly how I like it.

"Of course I'm okay. Why wouldn't I be okay? What makes you think I'm not okay?" I babbled and then took a swig of coffee to stop the babbling.

He grinned. "Well, alright then. All is well. Let's go out on an actual date."

"Actual date?" I sprayed out the coffee I just sipped on to his white T-shirt. *Kill me now.*

Beau continued, unperturbed. "You know, with a meal and maybe a movie. You've been on a date before, haven't you?" He set the plates of *pain perdu* on the table, grabbed his coffee, and sat next to me at the breakfast bar.

"Of course, it has just been a ... while." I started dribbled syrup over my *pain perdu.*

He shook his head and sprinkled his *pain perdu* with powdered sugar. "Define awhile." He leaned back and sipped his coffee.

I took a bite, hummed my approval, and considered. "Since before my marriage."

"Doug-ass." He scoffed.

"Yep, he did not want to waste any money and why should he when I can work all day and then cook all his meals at night?"

"You cook?" He dug into his *pain perdu.*

I shook my head and chewed. "Not anymore. Too many negative associations." I slashed at my meal with fervor.

"Not a problem. I'm an excellent chef."

I lowered my utensils and inhaled. "Beau, you know there's a problem."

"What problem Shell? We like each other, we are both consenting adults. What's the issue?" He took another bite and then sipped on his coffee.

"My reputation, the fact that, for all intents and purposes, I'm banging the help."

"I am not the help. I am the concierge and just taking care of your needs." He raised his eyebrows lasciviously, and I chuckled.

I blinked. "Ok, that was dirty in a good way."

"See, that is how I know you're the girl for me. You know that there is a good dirty and a bad dirty. Although we should really try them both out. Now come here."

$$\text{---} \maltese \text{---}$$

21

The Morning After

Beau

I went in for a kiss and then stabbed a piece of her French toast, dipped it in syrup and fed it to her. "You get grumpy if you don't eat. Don't make any decisions about us until you finished your meal. Orange juice?"

She rolled her eyes but then said, "Yes, please."

"See, already less grumpy."

She frowned at me, then shrugged and added more syrup to her *pain perdu*. "So, what is on the agenda today?"

"First, we check on the Littles, see if your mom can watch them, and then head to the hospital to see about Gelly and Alex."

"But first we finish this meal!" Shell dug into her French toast.

"Yes, priorities."

After a peaceful breakfast, she grabbed her clothes and ran to the bathroom to change while I changed in the bedroom. We made our way to the main house via the side door.

Valerie warmly greeted us at the door with a hug. "Madame, you weren't there went I woke up. I was worried."

"Sorry Valerie." Shell hugged her back.

"It's okay. Ms. Ellie Mae told us you were having a sleepover with M. Beau."

Shell attempted to clear her throat. "Uhh."

"Here baby, have a coffee." Ms. Ellie Mae appeared at the doorway and handed Shell the cup and a lifeline.

"Thanks," she told her. "I need to call Mrs. Mouillé to let her know she will be in charge of L'Académie for a few days." Shell then scurried into the house.

"Coward," Ms. Ellie Mae and I said in unison.

"Beau, dear, Mr. Bruce wanted you to take your coffee and meet him on the front porch." She handed me a cup as well and with a steely glint and a "bless your heart," and flounced away. We were totally busted.

This was not good. Although, if I were a parent and someone slept with my unmarried daughter under my roof; I'd have met them at the door with my shotgun. No firearms were visible when I entered the patio. That was a good sign ... right? Just Mr. LeBlanc rocking in a rocking chair and sipping his coffee.

"Beau."

"Mr. LeBlanc," I said, thinking the occasion warranted more formality.

With a wave towards the porch swing, he said, "Have a seat."

In hindsight, sitting on the porch swing that Shell and I cuddled up on the last night might not have been a wise choice.

"I'm an old-fashioned man, Beau." He looked out on to his front yard garden.

"Yes, sir." Because, really, what else could I say?

"And being an old-fashioned man, I'm not okay with men sleeping with my unmarried daughter. I consider that disrespectful. Are you disrespectful, son?"

"No, sir." I slouched forward, chin to my chest.

He took a knife and a small branch from his pocket and started whittling. "That's what I thought. How long have you known my daughter now, Beau?"

It did not look that dangerous. Still, it paid to stay alert. "It has been over two months, sir."

"That is not a long time."

"No, sir."

"Sometimes you just know." He kept whittling.

"Yes, sir."

Then he glared at me. "Nevertheless, I don't recall you courting my daughter at all. Have you taken her out to dinner?"

"No, sir."

"Movies, dancing, even breakfast?" he asked.

"No, sir."

"Now, Beau, I'm not telling you how to run your love life. I'm just telling you, you have to do better. You don't want me to think that you're using my daughter and disrespecting her."

Oh, God, kill me now. "No, sir."

"Excellent, because my wife is right now on the phone with your mama, and I have a feeling that you are going to hear this lecture again. But I'm not going to experience what I did this morning again, am I?"

"No, absolutely not sir."

"Because emotions were running high last night, I'm letting it slide. You saved my Shell's life and for that I thank you. But my daughter is a worthy and beautiful soul, don't you agree?"

"Absolutely."

"And she deserves to be treated with love and respect. Throughout her first marriage, I witnessed the disrespect she endured. I tried to let them work it out and stay out of the way. That won't happen a second time. Do you hear what I'm saying?" And Mr. Bruce reached behind his rocker and pulled out his shotgun. He started calmly polishing it.

Shit. "Yes, sir, absolutely, sir. It will never happen again."

"That's what I thought. Your mama raised you right. Don't disappoint her."

Catholic guilt is an art form. "No, sir." Then we just sat there in very uncomfortable silence while he cleaned his gun. Finally, Mr. LeBlanc set the gun aside and made to get up.

"Now I'm going to get another cup of coffee, and you best be going about your business. Hopefully, we will never speak of this again."

"Yes, sir … I mean… no sir."

Mr. LeBlanc nodded and walked back in as Shell walked back out. She gave me a hug and asked, "How bad was it?"

"Well, my little coward, his shotgun is nice and clean and apparently your mother is calling my mother."

"Oh, crap." She pulled away, but I kept her next to me.

"Not an issue. He is right. I need to court you."

"Court me?"

I nodded. "Absolutely, you deserve the whole shebang, flowers, dinner, movies, little gifties. Get yourself prepared to be wooed."

"Seriously?" Shell scoffed. "Aren't we beyond that?"

"Nope, but before that. Let's go check on Gelly and Alex. You ready to go?"

"Let me grab my purse." While Shell grabbed her purse, I said my goodbyes to the Littles and the LeBlancs and escaped to my truck. When Shell approached, I skirted around my truck to open her door. Mr. LeBlanc nodded from the window.

"So, I can't open doors for myself anymore?" she asked as I hoisted her up into the seat.

"Nope, it is all part of the courting process. Also, you get to choose a playlist for the drive to Lafayette. Our Lady hospital is about an hour away. Have at it." I gestured to the stereo. When the synthesizers started playing, I cringed. "What's this?"

"Cool for cats. Seemed appropriate, since this morning was kinda surreal."

I shook my head and kept driving. "Our current predicament makes you think about being bitter and a nasty little rash?"

"Well, it isn't a documentary," she huffed. "Fine, I'll change it."

More synthesizers. Shell smiled.

Only you by Yaz. Well, alright then. I truly only needed the love she gave. That could help my wooing. Then I grinned, what if 'our song' was eighties alt rock music?

Michelle

While my mom watched the Heberts and tattled on Beau to Ms. Denise, we headed to the hospital listening to the best of the eighties music. We got there on *Strange Love* by Depeche Mode.

"OKaaay." Beau turned off the stereo, but then my phone just kept singing of pain. I bit on my lips to keep from laughing when I turned it off. "Remind me to think twice about giving you free rein on the musical selections during future road trips."

"I have eclectic tastes." I blinked as I thought about them and then shook my head.

When I opened my eyes, Beau was right there in front of me. "Really, tell me more about that."

I stifled my smile and shook my head. "I don't think so."

He rounded the truck, opened my door, and lowered me to the ground. "Remind me to have the blinking discussion with you."

I made a beeline for the hospital. "The blinking discussion? What you are talking about?"

"What indeed." He caught up to me and opened the hospital door for me.

Gelly seemed much improved when we arrived at her room. The burns were hardly visible as doctors wrapped her left side near the ear. Clearly, the rafter damaged more on her neck and torso than her face. Her neck, torso, and left arm were bandaged.

"I'm so sorry Gelly!" I told her. "How are you feeling?"

"Some pain, because they are going light on the meds, but that means I can think. Thanks for making sure they discussed that with me, Beau."

"I knew what you wanted, and I just told them." He leaned down and kissed her forehead.

"Have you been to see Alex?" I asked.

"Yes, every few hours, they roll me over to him. We visited all morning long. There is some movement on the brain scan, but he hasn't woken up. I feel so guilty. It was always a risk in my profession, but I'm so sorry that Alex had to suffer. He will pull out of it. You'll see." Gelly's voice cracked.

Placing my hand on her shoulder, I let her know, "My whole family is praying for him, Gelly. We are fixin' to visit him now. You want to come?"

"Yes." We had to get an orderly to help put Gelly into a wheelchair so as not to aggravate her burns.

We entered Alex's room to an eerie stillness, save for the persistent beeping of the medical apparatus. Gelly clasped Alex's hand with her uninjured hand, resulting in a noticeable blip on the heart rate monitor. A good sign. At least Gelly had hope to sustain her. She looked at me.

"We wasted time, Alex and I. We wanted to do things. I wanted to have children, but he didn't, really. I should have insisted. We always danced. Did I tell you that? That was our celebration. I love dance, and he learned every style so we could share that."

Beau went up to her and kissed her on the forehead again. "We'll leave you alone."

"You saw the blip, though, right?"

I nodded. "Absolutely. Alex knows you're near. Talk to him."

Just as we were leaving, Etienne arrived. "How is he?"

"No change," I said. "But Gelly is doing better." Etienne nodded and looked in on them.

Gelly was staring daggers at him. "What are you doing here!?"

"I came to check on you both," he said. "And I have some—"

"—Get out. Teche News reported you went after the second shooter. You knew Alex was down and instead of helping him, you chased after that bastard who helped Doug."

"Gelly, that was after we got Alex to the ambulance, and that bastard was shooting at you and the kids. He was an immediate threat."

"Don't call me Gelly! You could have gotten Alex help faster. I don't want to talk to you or see you!" She turned her back to him.

"He's my cousin Gel ... Angelle. I didn't want anything to happen to him." Etienne pleaded from the doorway.

The ruckus caused the floor nurse to intervene. "Sir, you'll have to leave. It is not healthy to rile the patients." Etienne nodded and then gestured for us to follow him out.

I turned to Gelly. "We'll be right back, Gelly. Do you want something from the cafeteria?"

"Can you bring me a coffee? The stuff the nurses provide is swill."

"Sure thing," I promised, and we left with Etienne.

"What's wrong?" Beau asked.

"We followed the perp. He was hiding out at the old Chretien point plantation."

"The one with the Tera stairs?" I asked.

"The what?" Etienne frowned.

"The stairs that Vivien Leigh came down were based on the ruins of that plantation in *Gone with the wind*." I explained.

"I don't know. The old run down plantation by Sunset."

I nodded. "That's the one."

"Anyway! We found the remains of a camp. Someone had been living on the land, but we found something else … or rather someone else."

"No!" Shaking my head in denial.

"I'm sorry Michelle. It was the remains of Valerie Hebert. The Heberts are officially orphans."

"I'll adopt them!" I declared, pleading up at Beau. "We promised them they would not go into foster care or be separated."

"That is fine, Shell, but these things take time. In the interim, we need to find them a foster home, hopefully one that will keep them together," Beau said.

"We'll take them!" Denise Babineaux came in with her high heels and perfectly coiffed hair. "Herman and I applied for foster care when we learned about the Heberts. We figured with our own children on their own, our big empty house could help needy children. We received our approval last week, so we will take them."

I ran over to Ms. Denise and gave her the biggest hug I could. "Thank you, thank you."

"There, there, baby." Ms. Denise cooed, embracing me while staring daggers at her son. I guess my mom already called her. I didn't care. Ms. Denise could scold away as far as I was concerned, as long as we saved those Littles. "Now you go with Beau to get coffee and pastries. You can discuss, what do you young people call it, logistics?"

I walked toward Beau. "We need to get Gelly some decent coffee, too."

"My Herman already took care of that." He held up the Café Rêve bag he had. "The cafe is right there at the River Ranch development. Go grab a cup of coffee or tea and brainstorm ways to minimize the trauma for those poor babies. And you..." she looked over at Etienne, "I don't remember if I thanked you for saving my baby and Alex."

"I'm pretty sure Angelle doesn't see it that way. In fact, I know she doesn't. But she is going to need protection. From what I understand, she witnessed the second shooter."

"Give her time. She needs to recuperate, and the love of her life is still in danger. Patience, Etienne. Gelly is warm-hearted and intelligent. Give things time to settle. We will make sure we watch over Gelly. Now you go get the bastard who did this."

"That is my plan, ma'am." Ms. Denise kissed his cheek and shooed us all away.

Once at the truck, Beau asked me, "Where to now?"

"I'm doing what your mama told me to. Besides, a tall glass of Voodoo iced coffee from Rêve, sounds delicious."

"Goat's milk, molasses, and cold brew. What's not to like?" We headed to Rêve and ordered two Voodoo iced coffees and two pastries. Once they were done, we carried our order outside and sat on the patio. I just took a deep breath. I needed to get back to school. As the director, I had myriad responsibilities. For now, I would rely on my competent staff to handle everything in my absence. Plus, as Ms. Denise sensed, I needed time to relax and decompress.

22

Une tasse de cafe [A cup of coffee]

Beau

Mixing the goat's milk and Steen's syrup into my voodoo coffee concoction, I took my first tasty sip. "Should we talk now?"

"No, let's enjoy first. We can talk about serious stuff later. For now, let's just have a little downtime. Time for some small talk. Tell me about yourself, Beau. What are your favorite foods?" She mixed hers as well, and then we alternated between sipping and talking.

"Define foods," I said, sipping my coffee.

"Cold day foods." Shell took a bite of her scone.

"Gumbo."

She nodded as she finished chewing. "Correct answer. What kind of gumbo?"

Hah! Gumbo was the correct answer. "Chicken and sausage."

She shrugged. "My favorite is seafood, but it's too pricey."

"I thought you got paid very well."

Giving an exaggerated frown, she pointed at me. "Hey! Teacher dinners out and the school pantry, remember? We all gotta have a hobby, and mine is expensive."

"I don't know if school supplies and staff rewards count as a hobby."

She waved that away. "Different strokes, next question ... favorite dessert?"

With my eyes closed, I could almost taste it. "Doberge from Pouparts. White cake with chocolate frosting. My mom always buys me a doberge cake for my birthday."

"Yummy! Ms. Denise is the best."

"No argument there. What about you? What is your favorite dessert?"

"I love that layered cake, but I would have to say Cream Cheese King Cake from Keller's Bakery. Plus, Mardi Gras, is my all-time favorite holiday season."

"Excellent answer." By this time, we finished our pastries. "Last question before the 'logistical planning' starts," she said.

"Shoot."

"Why no girlfriend or wife? You gave me the yadda yadda yadda version, but I want more details."

"Like I said, it didn't work while I was in the Marines. A family has always been my dream to the point that I built a house on Babineaux land with four bedrooms because I wanted tons of kids. Long-distance relationships did not work for me. After being burned a few times, I realized it just wasn't in the cards. Let's just say I now have trust issues. And you?"

"Trust and time. While I was married to Doug-ass, I was just teaching regular old first grade. Then I got a chance to see an immersion program. They have one in Lafayette where the entire school is French Immersion. It was amazing. Using my 'kitchen French' that my family always spoke, I earned a scholarship for teachers to perfect my French. After a summer spent Nova Scotia learning French while Doug cheated on me, I washed that man right out of my hair. After that the progress was became a French Immersion teacher, master's, doctorate in administration and then Académie school director. It took a long time to finish my training, so ... no time for dating."

"And now, do you have time for dating?"

She blinked, and I watched until she opened her eyes. "Weren't we supposed to be talking about logistics?"

I leaned forward, my elbows on the table. "First, let's talk about blinking."

"Everybody blinks," she hedged.

"Then I'll just infer what you mean by blinking. Bet I'm not far off the mark." I smiled, stared at her mouth, and imagined kissing her. Within a few moments, she closed her eyes and smiled softly. "No one blinks like you, Shell," I chuckled.

"Logistics, Beau," she insisted.

"By all means." I told her and then cleared my brain so I could think. "First, we need to get the Littles from your mom. We will tell them that my parents will be fostering them together, to ease their biggest worry. Then we'll bring them to my parents' house."

Shell tapped her fingers on the table. "Is there room for me at your parents'?"

"Yes, you think you should go with them?"

She nodded. "I'm the person they have known and trusted the longest. We could then bring them to school together until they catch that maniac. I don't want to let down our guard." After that, Shell enjoyed the last dregs of her Voodoo cafe.

"Good point. The fact is, I already asked my parents, and they said that you're more than welcome."

"They are the best, you know." She stacked the plates and cups for the server to pick up. "Before we get the Littles, I think we should set up the rooms for them."

"They'll probably want to sleep in your room." Since we'd already paid, we headed back to the truck.

"Fine, but when they are not sleeping, I want them each to have a space. We also need to keep badge day going. I think they really like that."

"Let me check with Etienne." I opened her door and boosted her in. Then I quickly texted Etienne.

> Badge day continues at my parent's house on Saturdays

Before I could close the door, Etienne texted back.

> Etienne: Roger that

When I showed the Etienne's response, she smiled and asked, "Maybe we could do it at the school and invite more kids?"

I held up my hands. "Slow down ... let's first get over this crisis."

Once we got on the road, Shell continued our discussion. "Right. So, Monday- Friday school, badge day on Saturday and church on Sunday. What about when I have to work late? Should our parents watch them?"

"Nope." I shook my head, refusing to lower our guard again. "They stay with us. I'm not letting any of you out of my sight."

She smiled at that. "Ok, that covers it."

"Nearly."

She cocked her head to the said, "What's left?"

"Date night."

"Date night?"

Eyes on the road, I nodded. "Yes, when you and I have adult time, and I court you."

"Why do we need that?"

"One because I really like you, hence last night's activities, and two, because you deserve some courting. Plus," I grinned, "it will be fun."

"Fun?"

"Yes, fun. You remember fun, don't you?"

Shell grimaced. "Vaguely. I don't know if I liked it that much."

"Then you clearly were doing it wrong." We merged back onto Highway LA 31 to pick up the Littles from her parent's house.

"What about the kids? We can't expect your parents to guard them all the time."

"They will watch them, not guard them. Armand is staying with me, and until he deploys, he can guard them during our dates."

"How far is it from your place to your parents'?"

"About a two-minute walk, across a field, inside our fence. You didn't notice the house across the way when you were earning your horsemanship badge?"

"Yes, but I figured it was a big bunkhouse or a relative's property."

"It is a relative, their son. Gelly and Alex's place is on the property as well, but not visible from my parents' house."

"Oh, I'd love to see your house. I mean, you toured my fancy garage apartment."

"That can be arranged as part of the whole courting ritual. So, which night works best for you?"

"Ah ... Tuesday? Wait, did I agree to courting?"

"Let's say you tentatively agreed and that you are still processing all the information. I'll ask you each time, and you can always tell me 'no'. We will start slow. How about this upcoming Tuesday? How does pizza and a movie sound?"

"That actually sounds like ... fun."

"See courting. It's painless, not even a pinch." Shell blinked again.

"You're killing me Shell!" But I couldn't think about it now, we had Littles to help.

Moving the Heberts to my parents was seamless. When we mentioned I lived nearby and that Shell was also moving in, they visibly relaxed. Once we arrived at my parents' house, they explored both their rooms and Shell's. She explained that before they went to bed, she'd have read aloud and hot chocolate time in her room. Then she explained 'tranquility time' when they could play quietly, nap, or read each afternoon after school. We told them it was tranquility time now, so we let them hang out in their rooms. Then the time came to tell them.

"I really don't know how to do this," I admitted.

"We'll just rip the bandaid off." She called the Littles into the living room and gathered them close to her on the couch and then she told them. "We have some bad news my loves ..."

It was gut wrenching, but I'm glad Shell was there. Valerie and Bailey Marie were holding on to her and sobbing. Tanner looked like he was trying to hold it back. He did not want to cry in front of his sisters. "Wanna go for a walk?" I asked him. He nodded, and I took his hand and led him outside. As soon as the porch door closed, tears started streaming down Tanner's face.

"I'm the man of the house," Tanner said.

"No, you're a six-year-old child. Leave this to me. I'll make sure you are taken care of."

"But foster care is temporary. We might have to leave. I need to learn more to help take care of my family."

"Madame Michelle is making sure you still have badge earning workshops every Saturday, but I promise I *will* be there for you. This doesn't fall on your shoulders, Tanner."

Tanner looked skeptical. "You can't promise that."

"I can and I do." And that was my instant epiphany that the Heberts and Shell were mine to protect. I knew exactly what I wanted. Now, I just had to convince Shell. The Littles were key.

I walked Tanner back after a bit of silent contemplation. I handed him over to Shell and his sisters, went back outside for some privacy, and called up Etienne. "Who do I contact about adopting the Heberts?"

"A single man adopting three children. That might be an issue."

"Well, my goal is to not be single much longer."

"So it's that way, huh? I kinda had a feeling. Does Michelle know anything about this?"

"About the adoption or about the impending nuptials?"

"Either, both?"

I shook my head. "Nope."

"So, starting strong."

"I'm starting with a date."

"Cool, just tell me when and I'll hang out with Armand so we can watch the Littles."

"Tuesdays."

"We'll be there."

Michelle

After school, during the Littles' tranquility time, I had coffee on the porch with Ms. Denise and my mama. It was relaxing to just sit on the rockers and porch swings and enjoy the moment. When Beau was there, he kept an eye on things from his porch. If not, then Armand would be around.

Today we were meeting up with Renee, Ms. Denise's niece, and Beau's cousin. She had brought by a condolence gift basket for the Littles. They had received several of them since the funeral. "I hope they are doing better. It broke my heart watching them at the funeral. How long are you fostering them?" Renee asked, handing over a basket.

Ms. Denise answered, "Well, Mr. Herman and I are fostering them, but Michelle wants to adopt them. Really, they think of her as their mother, anyway. She reads to them at night and tucks them in. They move to her bed in the middle of the night. Then she wakes them up in the morning and gets them ready for school."

"Will it be hard to adopt them, you know, as a single mom?" Renee asked. Ms. Denise and my mama made snorting sounds.

"No, I can do it alone." More snorting noises ensued while I calmly sipped my coffee and ignored them.

"Have you tried doing it alone?" Renee took a sip of her coffee, "Cuz it seems like you have a lot of help with them here."

"You know, you ask a lot of questions for someone I barely know." Someone chortled.

"I'm nosy that way." Renee grinned and then added more sugar to her coffee.

I turned the tables on her. "Let me ask you a question. Did Beau talk to you about joining my faculty?"

"I'm not fluent enough in French," Renee grumbled.

"Did he talk to you about teacher scholarships to Ste. Anne in Nova Scotia?"

"Yes, I'm looking into it. My turn. So, you like my cousin?"

"Yes." I turned away from her to look at the horizon and sip my coffee in peace.

Renee grinned. "Not chatty, are you? How much do you like him?"

"Enough to sleep with him," my mama helpfully interjected. I glared at her, but she just sipped her brew.

"You're sleeping with him while you are fostering children?" Renee crinkled her nose.

"No, I slept with him one time. The night he saved us from the fire. He hasn't even mentioned it since then."

"Because Bruce had a 'come to Jesus' with him," my mama added, her mouth twitching.

"And because you are living under his mama's roof now," Ms. Denise, the other partner on this parental tag team, added, grinning over her coffee cup.

"Or maybe he is just not interested in me in that way," I countered.

This brought hoots of laughter. "Hardly," Ms. Denise said. "My boy is gone over you."

"Hmph." I focused my sight across the field to his home.

That's when Gelly walked over from her tiny home. Although she had healed enough to go home, she continued to spend most of her time at the hospital watching over Alex. She climbed the steps and smiled when she saw Renee.

"Gelly!" Renee ran over to give her two air kisses. "We have a question requiring your expertise."

"Really? Shoot." She smiled.

"As a social worker, who stands a better chance of adopting a child: a single mother or a married couple?" Renee asked, glancing pointedly at me.

"A married couple. There are more people to watch over the child or children, and if they both work, more money to support the family unit."

"I want to adopt them," I said.

"Ok, it could happen, but you wouldn't have priority," Gelly added.

"How could I get priority?" I asked.

"Get married," they all chorused.

"It is too soon," I insisted.

"Maybe, but you don't know if someone is going to petition to be the guardians of your little crew. I would do it sooner rather than later," Gelly warned.

"Do you love him?" Ms. Denise asked.

"I don't know. How would I know?"

"Imagine him gone and out of your life. Imagine him injured. Does it feel like your world is crumbling?" Gelly asked. I got up and hugged her.

"I'm sorry Gelly, and yes, if what happened to Alex had happened to Beau, I would be a basket case ... Oh no!"

"Oh yes," Renee responded.

"Hold on." I went to leave the room.

"Where are you going?" Renee asked.

"To check on flights to Las Vegas and tacky wedding chapels."

"No, ma'am," my mama and Ms. Denise said in unison.

My mama continued, "You let us take care of the details. You just get Beau to propose."

"Gah! What? No! How?" I babbled.

"The sooner the better, honey," my mama added. "When is your next date with Beau?"

"Tomorrow. It is some kind of surprise he is cooking up."

"Piece of king cake," Gelly said. "Get the big bad Marine to admit he has a weakness for you and get him to propose at the same time."

"Well, shit."

"Language!" the mothers chorused.

23

Date, Proposal, Proposal

Beau

With a sigh, I pinched the bridge of my nose because I was running late for our date. Starting the date with an annoyed Shell was not, as my mama would say, a propitious start. Fiddling with the ring in my pocket, I relaxed thinking about how happy Mawmaw Babineaux had been when she gave it to me. It was her engagement ring, the one she kept on a chain around her neck. The ring had an old-fashioned charm, with delicate engravings on the inside that read *Toujours* [forever] in French, a detail I knew Shell would appreciate.

Pulling into our driveway, my parents and Shell's parents were having daily afternoon cafe sur la galerie. [porch coffee] As I climbed the porch stair, it was obvious that my mom had let Ms. Ellie Mae in on my evening plans.

"Afternoon, Beau, such beautiful weather. And what are your plans for the evening?" I smiled, and Shell looked confused at such a stilted conversation from her mom.

"I'm doing well Ms. Ellie Mae. Shell and I have reservations at Jolie Blonde restaurant for this evening."

"That sounds nice! Maybe we should all go." Clearly, secrecy was a challenge for them. Note to self, must play poker or Bourré with them one day.

"Mom! It's a date. You can't invite yourself along on our date."

My cousin Renee was there as well. Shell would often talk about her 'evil' plan to lure Renee away from her school.

"Renee." I tipped my head to her.

"I'm here in case you agreed to the whole group date with your parents. I was called to babysit." Reveling in her Schadenfreude, she snickered.

I shook my head. "Yeah, not going to happen." Armand snorted from the front lawn. Renee glared at him. Armand was being used for muscle on the front lawn to prepare for tomorrow's crawfish boil. Officially, a social gathering; secretly, an engagement celebration. At least, that's what I hoped.

Reaching for her hand, I said, "C'mon Shell, let's get out of here."

"We could stay here and eat. I mean, if your parents want to spend more time with us."

"That would be wonderful. I already prepared a pot roast," my mom said, clearly wanting to see the proposal.

"Dates," I said, "do not include family, friends, and children." Then I whispered in Shell's ear. "I want you all to myself, Shell, please!" Yep, I had resorted to begging.

"I get to choose the music," she negotiated. Resigning myself to listening to weird music for a half hour, I nodded, and we said our goodbyes.

"Renee seems to be coming over a lot more." We held hands as we walked to my truck.

"My master plan to lure her away from her school is coming to fruition. Mwa ha ha!" When I cocked my head and furrowed my brows, she added, "What? That is my Dr. Evil imitation."

Shaking my head, I said, "More like his Mini-me." Then I boosted her into my truck.

"Hey, don't start the late date with short jokes! Also, don't knock the comic villain. In this crazy world, what sane person hasn't thought about having just a smidge of total global domination ... just for a while to fix all the flaws in the world?"

"This is true." I closed the door.

By the time we got on the road, synthesizer rock was already blasting from her phone, just waiting to hook up to my stereo.

"Wait, is this in French?"

Shell grinned. "Mylene Farmer. This is her rendition of a Baudelaire poem."

"Baudelaire?"

"You know, from the *Fleurs du mal,* the one that warns readers not to read his book. He was inspired by Edger Allen Poe."

"So creepy date music." Turning the truck towards Lafayette. *Not propitious at all.*

"More like eclectic music." She plugged in her phone as we started down the highway.

"Did she just say 'Die old man, it is too late?'"

"Well, it was more like 'Die Old Coward.'"

Rubbing the newly burgeoning pain in my temple, I snarked, "Definitely date music."

Shell stared down the road. "Well, it underlines that you need to live your life. The clock is ticking and that you shouldn't chicken out or you will die with regrets."

"Food for thought," or rather, exactly what I needed to hear.

A half hour later, I pulled into the Jolie Blonde parking lot and ran around to open Shell's door. "C'mon, let's have fun and not waste our time." She smiled at me then, like a teacher who just taught you something. Perhaps she had.

The food was superb, and the drinks were fun. The bartender, Seth, was a gem. You told him what you were feeling or what you were celebrating, and he created the perfect drink.

Shell told him, "I need a drink to ponder my possibilities," which was intriguing. Seth created a simmering phoenix cocktail, which was served flaming and which changed colors.

"You are a gift to mankind!" Shell beamed at him.

My turn. "Do you have some liquid courage?" Seth glanced over at Shell, winked at me, and then poured me some sixteen-year-old Lagavulin.

"Perfect," I told him and brought my drink to the table.

"Looks kinda boring compared to my multicolored, flaming selection."

"Because you are all color and I am staid."

"Hardly." Shell sipped and looked to the side. Oh, oh, something was on her mind. The moment had arrived. I needed to ask her now. "Can we talk?" she began. *Drat, too late.*

"Of course, that's what dates are for." Sitting, I took a sip of my liquid courage.

"We should get married." I was about to say 'that was my line,' when she continued. "If you think about it, it is the logical move."

"Logical?" *What was happening?*

"Gelly believes that as a married couple, we would have an easier time adopting the Heberts." She touched one finger.

"Okay." *How had this conversation gotten away from me so quickly?*

She babbled on. "And you can't deny that there is an attraction between us. You nearly kiss me senseless every night and then there was our one night together." She touched a second finger, but I lost my train of thought as I remember that night and her and us. "So, based on our goals, our compatibility, and that attraction," she enumerated all this with more fingers … like it was one of her stupid school checklists. "Plus, if we want to repeat that night together," which I absolutely wanted to, "we have to be mindful of not being seen as a negative influence on the children. Thus, I think we should get married."

"So, marrying me meets all of your checklist requirements?" Shell nodded. My jaw clenched. "What about love?"

Her face paled. "What?"

I took a slow sip of my scotch, set it down, and asked, "Do. You. Love. Me?"

"Well, I, I, I." she stuttered.

"Don't you think a discussion of marriage, a proposal of marriage, should mention love?" I was on the edge and needed to leave. "Check please!" Silence reigned at the table. I was glaring at Shell as she fidgeted in her chair. When the check arrived, I threw cash on the table, grabbed her hand, and then dragged her to the truck. We drove home in silence. I couldn't think. Everything was racing. Our end goals aligned, but it hurt being a means to an end. *End goal is the same*, I reminded myself.

Upon arrival, I rounded the truck and helped her down. She always smelled so damn good, but I refused to be distracted from my fury. As I walked her up the stairs, I pulled the ring out of my pocket, torn between handing it to her and throwing it at her. At the top of the stairs, I had decided. "Yes," I snarled.

"Yes, what?"

"Yes, I will marry you." Grabbing her hand, I shoved the ring on her finger. "Oh, and by the way, I love you, you impossible woman!" With an "Argh!" I turned, stomped down the stairs, and crossing the lawn to my house.

Michelle

When I walked in the house after the 'proposal gone wrong,' both my mama and Ms. Denise were still there. Their gazes flickered to my ring finger, confirming that both knew about Beau's impending proposal. And yet ... neither of them of them warned me.

"Hurray! Wedding planning time!" my mama celebrated.

"You could have told me, you know," I said, aggravated at how wrong it had gone.

"Why? Clearly you're in love and marrying him fits with your agenda." Flinging myself into the recliner, I hung my head down and massaged my temples. My mom, knowing me well, knew something was up. "Michelle Lynn LeBlanc! What did you do? I know that face! What did you do?"

"Nothing, I was honest with Beau, explained my 'agenda' as you call it, and asked him to marry me for a number of very logical reasons. Beau did not appreciate my logic."

"You're right Ellie Mae. She is the smartest idiot I have ever met," Ms. Denise told her and sat on the sofa next to me.

"Hey, I thought you were both on my side."

Ms. Denise reached over and rubbed my forearm. "Honey, I'm never on the side where you break my son's heart. So, spill, what happened?"

"Well, since I did not know that Beau was proposing," I glared at them, "I had some liquid courage..."

My mama plopped down next to Ms. Denise. "Oh Lord, help us when she makes drunk decisions."

"Mother, I was not drunk. I had a single drink, and then I explained to Beau all the excellent and logical reasons for us to marry."

"I bet that went over like a lead balloon," Ms. Denise snarked.

"Yeah, he pretty much yanked me out of the restaurant, gave me the silent treatment all the way home, then…"

"Then?" they both asked in chorus.

"Then he snarled, 'yes', shoved this ring on my finger, told me 'I love you, you impossible woman', and then stomped over to his house."

Both parental units were biting their lips to stifle their amusement. Glancing at the ring, then at me, they burst into gales of laughter, even some unladylike snorting. I narrowed my eyes at them.

"Well, in my defense, at least he said yes." More laughter. "He said I was an impossible woman!"

"He's right," my mother said. My mother!

"He also said he loves you, darling," Ms. Denise pointed out.

"I guess." They both brushed that aside. Ms. Denise crossed to the credenza, rifled through a drawer, and retrieved a yellow legal pad and a pen.

"So, we have a wedding to plan," she said.

"When do you want to get married, hun?" my mama asked.

"The sooner the better. We both want to adopt the Heberts and being married would look better on application."

"Tell me you didn't tell my Beau that was a reason to get married." Ms. Denise shook her head.

"Well, it's true." Both women rolled their eyes.

"How about three weeks? I'll call Father LeBrun at St. Francis and make sure there's a date available. Saturday may not be available, though," my mother said.

"Whatever, any day is fine." They both shook their heads and Ms. Denise wrote the dates for that week down.

"Her enthusiasm is contagious," Ms. Denise sniped.

"It's not that." I sighed. "There's just so much going on. Do you think Father LeBrun could come here?"

"I'm sure he could. I'll ask." Ms. Denise noted. I sighed heavily, and Ms. Denise looked worriedly at my mama.

She reassured Ms. Denise. "Don't worry. She loves him. She just hates doing things wrong. It always makes her grouchy."

I lifted my head. "I did nothing wrong!"

"Oh, you purposely hurt my baby boy's feelings?" Ms. Denise's disappointed face reassembled my mother's to a frightening degree.

"No, of course not. How was I supposed to know he was planning to ask me? Besides, there's nothing wrong with having logical, rational reasons to marry." I think my mama whispered *'Idiot Savant'* under her breath, but I might have just been paranoid.

Unfazed, my mama took charge. "Denise, can you find the invitations? Just use one of those fancy websites."

"On it." Then Ms. Denise turned to me and said, "You, my dear, will need to get some shopping done. Perhaps take a day off from school?"

"I can shop on weekends and after school. What kind of shopping do I need to do?"

"What kind of shopping? Ellie Mae, really!"

"I know. I swear she knows what you're talking about. It is all that teaching that has pulled her entire focus."

I frowned at them. "We are working on our application to expand to middle school this week. I need to be there."

"Darling, you hire competent people, and you are probably just going to re-read and edit their work, whether or not you are there. Trust them to do their jobs, and you can look it over after."

"Fine, but I reiterate, what kind of shopping? This isn't a first marriage for me, so I don't need anything fancy."

"It is for my Beau. So you will need a beautiful dress and a wedding registry." Then she added, "Take Gelly. She can help you."

"That's probably best since my sisters are not in the area and will probably have to scramble just to make the wedding. I'll take Aurelie as well."

"I already texted your sisters," Mama said.

"Already? I just got engaged." But they were in planning mode and not paying any attention to me. I rose to head to my room. "Fine, I'll call Gelly and Aurelie about looking for dresses. Anything else?"

"Well, you might try apologizing to my boy and telling him how you really feel. Although, not tonight. He has probably started drinking and telling his woes to Armand. Text him and let him know you want to talk to him tomorrow morning."

24

The Talk

Beau

My morning started with regret and a *gueule de bois.*
[hangover] My jumbled memories included telling
Shell I loved her, but not much after that, except for annoyance.
When I trudged up the stairs to my parents' house, my mama
met me on the porch with two cups of coffee.

"Heard you screwed the pooch with your proposal." She
took a long dreg on her coffee and handed me the other cup.

"Actually, she did the proposing. She explained to me all the
logical reasons that we should marry and when I asked her if she
loved me, she started sputtering like she hadn't thought about
it. Hadn't. Thought. About. It."

Mama put her hand on my shoulder. "Ouch! But she had
thought about it. She discussed it with us the day before. You
just caught her off guard."

"Right!" I grunted. "At any rate, I told her yes and gave her
the ring that Mawmaw had given me and left before I said
something we would have both regretted."

"Yes, and I can tell from your crazy hair and blood-shot eyes you went straight to bed after that. So you could contemplate how to convince her she is in love with you."

"Not quite," Armand scoffed as he came up the steps behind me. "Your coffee is better than his, especially this morning, Ms. Denise. Can I steal a cup?"

"Armand, *mon cher,* [my dear] whenever you want coffee, come over and I'll fix you a cup."

"Thank you, Ms. Denise, and to answer your question, he went home, got stinking drunk and then moaned about his love life. What's he is bellyaching about? He has an intelligent, beautiful, and kind woman that has agreed to marry him."

They both shook their heads at me as if *I* had done something wrong. "You don't understand!"

"Why you mad, M. Beau?" Valerie asked from the screen door.

Not wanting to delve into the details, I simply told her, "Last night, I had an idea about how events would happen, but it didn't go as planned."

"Well, failure is normal, and Mme. Michelle alway says *Les fautes sont des flêches.* [errors are arrows] So, what did you learn from your failure?"

"I didn't fail, but I didn't the succeed the way I wanted to succeed." All three of them stared at me like I was a lunatic.

Valerie shook her head and reentered the house, slamming the screen door behind her and saying, "*Les adultes sont fous.*" [Adults are crazy]

Neither the slamming screen door nor the howling laughs from my mom and Armand were helping my throbbing head. Then Shell came out the door. Her locks were a mass of peaty scotch colored curls and they were bouncing around her head. A curl dangled tantalizingly on her cheek and I just wanted to tug on it so see it bounce in the light. Plus, she was wearing a sexy outfit with a floaty shirt with a bow tied right above her full breasts and flowy pants that cinched in at her waist. Those curves ... she was killing me. A glance at her finger verified that my grandma's ring was still there. A good sign, I think.

"Ms. Denise, Armand, breakfast is all ready. Do you mind if I speak with Beau alone? We have ... things to discuss."

Valerie interrupted from inside the house. "Careful Madame. He is in a weird mood. Getting what he wants seems to make him grumpy."

The corner of Shell's lips twitched, and my mood lightened. "I'll be extra careful. Thanks Valerie. Now go in and eat. Don't forget to help with the dishes and then help your brother and sister get dressed." Her teeth bit down on her plump bottom lip to hold on to a serious expression. Then she turned to me with her amber scotch eyes and said. "I'm sorry, Beau."

My chest tightened. "Sorry for what?"

She lifted her hand to my shoulder, hesitated, then placed it behind her back. "Beau, I didn't realize that you wanted to marry me. My logical reasoning was because I thought I needed to convince you. How could I have known that you wanted the same thing I wanted?"

"I'm not sure that we want the same things. At least, I'm not sure we want them for the same reasons. Do you just want to marry me for logical and practical reasons?"

Shell shook her head. "No, we have chemistry, Beau."

Squeezing the bridge of my nose, I said, "So logical and practical reasons plus lust. That's not enough."

"Fine! I love you too, you big idiot. The last time I told someone I loved him, it backfired on me big time."

I breathed a sigh of relief. "I'm not Doug-ass."

Inside, Ms. Ellie Mae complained, "Oh my God, they are both terrible at this."

"Seriously, now might not be the time to bring up her homicidal ex-husband. Where did I go wrong?" my mama added.

We both grinned at each other. "We are terrible at this," I said.

Shell drew her fingers through her curls. "Because we're both terrified. At least, I am. I'm scared to tell you I love you."

"I find it's easier and less scary if you yell at the object of your affection and then stomp off. Liquor also helps." I grinned.

"Good to know. So are we okay?" She held out her hand to me.

I grabbed her hand and pulled her to me. "Almost. Just need one more thing."

She grinned. "What is that?"

I whispered in her ear. "The blink. Please explain the blink to me."

Shell tucked her head into the crook of my neck and smiled against my skin. Then she whispered, "The blink is what I use to imagine the impossible, but stay content with the reality. I blink to think about things that I want but will never get, and then to put those thoughts behind me."

I tightened my hold on her. "Next time you blink, I want you to whisper what you want in my ear." She blinked again. I pulled her into a hug and leaned down to whisper in her ear. "Tell me!"

"After we get married," she whispered back. I hugged her tight and relented.

"Fine, I'll give you some time, but once we say I do, I claim all the blinks." She smiled at that.

"Deal! In the meantime, we need to shop for a wedding registry."

Shaking my head, I begged, "Ugh! No, don't make me do it!"

"It will be fun."

Armand yelled from the kitchen. "No, no, it won't"

Shell narrowed her eyes at the doorway. "Ignore him. Tomorrow after school. We'll go to Target."

"Nooo!" I moaned.

"They have both an electronics department and tools," she crooned as she ran her fingers through my hair to straighten it and kissed my forehead.

"Do they have registries at the hardware stores and auto mechanics shops?" I grumbled.

"No, but we can go and you can make a list of what you want. Plus, we need to sign up for the foster parenting classes. In case there is a delay in the adoption. That way, we can move the kids in when I move in." Her lips were featherlight on mine.

I deepened the kiss. When we came up for air, I asked, "How about we wait a week after the wedding before moving them in?"

She beamed. "Like a honeymoon?"

"Exactly."

Grinning, she pulled away and headed back in. "I can get behind that plan."

$$25$$

The Final Countdown

Michelle

The mothers decided they could plan a wedding in less than a month. Since they were doing most of the planning, we did not complain. Beau's marching order included inviting his friends to help ready his house for his new, expanded family. As I cleaned and organized in the living room, I could hear them teasing Beau as they assembled new beds and moved furnishings in the Littles' rooms.

"Marc, do you have any words of wisdom for Beau and his new ball and chain?" Etienne asked.

"Hey!" I yelled from the living room.

"I mean his beautiful new wife," Etienne yelled and then whispered, "who has bat-like hearing."

"I heard that too!"

"Which only proves me right," Etienne yelled back.

"Idiots," I whispered and when there was no response, I assumed it was because my hearing was more acute than theirs. I kept organizing and eavesdropping.

"Can you offer more help in the 'what to do with kids' department?" Beau asked

"You're great with the Littles," Armand said, using our nickname for them.

"In limited contexts with specific tasks, but this is parenting. It is 24/7."

"Well, make sure you spend time with them every day. Sophia and I have a special time every week. We call it Sophia Day." I could hear the smile in Marc's voice. Aww, he was adorable.

"Like alone time? What would we do?"

"Think about what they like and do those things with them," Marc suggested. "Sofia likes to have tea. We started out with fake tea parties where she would tell me about her day. Then my mom taught her how to make a proper pot of tea and how to make scones and tea sandwiches. Now on Sunday after church we put together a tea, and we can invite whomever we like to tea. You could do that. Just find out what each of them likes."

"Hey, how come you never invited us to tea?" Armand asked.

"Well, she invites a friend and since I want to listen in on her life, I usually am just there to interact with them and my mom."

"You don't think she wants to listen into your life?" Etienne asked.

"That's so sweet!," I said from the living room, "but I agree, invite someone to tea."

"Ears like a bat," Armand whispered. I walked to the bedroom and threw a throw pillow from the sofa at him. Laughter followed me out of the room.

The bedrooms were pretty nondescript, so I asked Ms. Denise to bring the Littles over to tell us their decor preferences. As they entered, I provided them with a sketch pad and colored pencils. Then I designated one person from Beau's Krewe to accompany each Hebert, allowing them to explore their rooms and discuss decor and paint preferences.

Dragging Beau to the living room couch for some alone time, I said, "Maybe the room decor will help you decide how you want to spend Val-day, Tan-day, and Bailey-day."

He pulled me closer to him. "Funny."

Making a circle with my finger, I got him to turn around so I could massage his shoulders. "I'm serious. You could take a day a month for each of them and a Shell-day, for me."

He looked over one shoulder. "Is there a Beau-day?"

With a sigh, I laid my head between his shoulder blades. "Absolutely! You want me to put squiggly, disgusting worms on a hook. I'm your girl."

He turned to face me and waggled his eyebrows. "I was thinking more of a weekend away each month with just the two of us."

I giggled. "Well then, Shell-day and Beau-day will always be together."

"I think this is the start of a beautiful marriage." He leaned down and kissed me lightly, and then the kiss transformed into something more. As we pulled apart, he channeled Rhett Butler, "You should be kissed often, and by me." I grinned because for our last two date nights, I had come over and we had sat on the couch and watched *Gone with the Wind*.

"That I should. Now keep getting the house ready while Gelly, Aurelie, and I do shop for decor and dresses." With that, I abandoned him for shopping with the girls.

It had been over a month since the fire. Gelly was still healing with bandages over her skin grafts on her face, arm, and torso. However, she had grown her auburn pixie cut out. With the turtleneck and long sleeves, only a small portion of the bandages was visible.

"How are you doing?" I asked Gelly.

"Ready to get out and indulge in some serious retail therapy?" she replied.

"Me too," added Aurelie.

This was new for me. During the school year, while I socialized with the teachers, staff, and parents, I rarely had time for anything else. We started the shopping expedition with coffee and pastries at Soleil cafe. *I need to play hooky more often.* I grinned as we loaded up my Volvo and headed to Lafayette for round one. Renee, whose aunt owned the *Au Bal* [to the ball] dress shop in Meauxville, said she would meet us there after school for round two.

"Decor for the rooms first." Distributing the Littles' sketches once we parked in front of the home and decor store, I explained the rules. "Find things that look like they go with your sketches. You have forty-five minutes and $100."

"Is this like a game show?" Gelly asked.

"Sort of, except that everyone wins and we don't spend all day shopping at one store. I will see you here by the patio furniture so we can check out in forty-five minutes. On your marks-"

Gelly and Aurelie both took off before I could finish counting down. Since I had already scoped out the store and knew precisely what I wanted and where to get it, I finished in less than twenty minutes. I purchased a coke, Dr. Pepper, and grinned evilly as I waited for my loser friends.

After grousing about how I cheated at the decor store, we purchased paint in the colors the Littles wanted at the paint store. We only purchased sample cans so the Littles could choose their final color. Then we headed to Beausoleil Books, where we also got them books based on their interests, because hello, two of the three of us were teachers.

Children's clothes shopping was next. This time the game would be more collaborative. "So, the object of the game is to choose a capsule wardrobe for each Hebert. We can use their favorite color as inspiration."

"Do you make a game out of everything?" Gelly asked.

Aurelie shushed her. "Shh! I need to know the rules so I can win this time."

"This is a win-win activity. We get a ten-minute timer and we each get clothes that will all go together for one child. Then we select the best of all they have gathered. The final wardrobe will have two outerwear pieces, six shirts, and five bottom pieces."

Getting clothes for them was a joy with so many cute kids' clothes. In the end, we bought each Little enough cute, inexpensive, and sturdy clothes to create a fabulous capsule wardrobe. These were versatile year-round wardrobe supplemented with either a few dresses or, for Tanner, a few suits for church and formal occasions. These shopping adventures went without incident because need help from store personnel. I couldn't say the same for the dress shopping.

Renee met us in Meauxville at the *Au Bal* dress shop door, and we decided not to eat lunch because the boutique said they would serve us champagne and sandwiches. That was mistake number one. They had only a few sandwiches, tomato and cucumber, nothing to sustain us. Because my sisters could not come until right before the wedding, I had made Aurelie my maid of honor, Gelly my matron of honor, and her cousin Renee, a bridesmaid. They would be helping me with preparation and organizing the rehearsal dinner. Aurelie had gotten my sisters' dress and shoe sizes, so our task was simply to choose dress styles. They knew we were shopping today and said they would text back with input on dresses we sent them.

"Oh, my God!" The sales consultant froze, and her mouth dropped open as she stared at Gelly's bandaged scars.

Wanting to hit first and ask questions later, I adulted and controlled my temper. "Is there a problem?"

She pointed at Gelly. "Well, she has bandages on."

"And?" Aurelie asked, not amused.

"Well, what if she gets blood on the dresses?"

Gelly, so much more mature than I, responded, "The bandages are to cover healing skin grafts. The grafts have healed already, but I want to protect them because we will be putting on and taking off dresses."

"Can't one of them try them on for you?" She gestured in our general direction. "Although you two are a lot bigger than her." She pointed to Renee and me. "But she," meaning Aurelie, "is nearly the same size."

"Are you related to the manager, by chance?" I asked, as it reminded me of Loser Jeremy once more.

"Yes, I'm a cousin."

"Yeah, get your cousin, please. I'd hate for her to lose out on the sale of six dresses because a relative pressured her into hiring from the 'Losers R Us' family employment agency'."

"Well, really!" And she stalked off.

"Don't pay any attention to her, Gelly. You're stunning and I'm so happy those grafts are healing well. Let's each select three dresses while we wait for the manager to come and apologize." I gave Gelly a hug and then we turned to scope out the dresses.

Renee was still indignant on Gelly's behalf. "She better be on her A game or I'll be talking to my Tante Em!" she fumed. We set aside six dresses to try for bridesmaids and three bridal gowns for me when a woman rushed over.

"Whatever Marlene told you, I apologize. Don't know how my sister talked me into hiring her. She will be the ruin of me."

Nodding solemnly, I commiserated. "I hear you. I've already had to deal with the backlash of being emotionally blackmailed into hiring loser relatives."

"Thank you for understanding. I'm Aimee, the manager. Welcome to *Au Bal* dress shop. Renee! Oh, no! Please don't get me in trouble with your aunt."

"Not your fault, Aimee. However, might I suggest Marlene work on inventory until she has acquired basic social skills? It's surprising I've never seen her around."

"I make it a point to make sure she is not around when your Aunt Em is working. You can imagine why."

"Indeed," Renee laughed. Aimee then took in the racks of dresses they had selected thus far.

"I didn't make your appointment," Aimee glared at the storage room, "but from the selections you've made, I'm guessing wedding and not some other event?"

"Correct, and we need a seamstress who can do alterations quickly, mostly before, but also on the day of the wedding."

"We have a seamstress in-house who can do that. Someone I'm not related to." We all snorted at that.

Aimee turned and smiled at them. She stopped smiling when she saw Gelly.

"You're Angelle Landry, I read the report in Teche News. You got hurt rescuing those three orphans." Gelly swallowed, but just nodded. "Thank God you were there. You look to be healing up nicely. How is your husband? The news reported that he was hurt as well."

Tears welled in Gelly's eyes. "He seems to be stable. He hasn't woken up yet."

"Oh sweety! I'll be praying for him. C'mon, let's do something stress-free and fun. Let's try on some dresses. I sent my useless cousin out to get us proper food. Also, you will be getting the family and friends rate on all of your dresses."

"You don't have to do that," I said.

"Don't think I don't know who you are, Madame LeBlanc. You were in that burning building with Mrs. Landry. Plus, you established our French Immersion school. Since L'Académie opened, at least ten families have moved back to Meauxville. This is a local business, and we can do our part as well. You get the friends and family discount. Now stop arguing so we can start trying on dresses!"

We selected perfect dresses for each of us. My bridal dress was an ivory chiffon empire-waisted dress with illusion of three-quarter length sleeves in a lovely lace. The only requirement that I had for the bridesmaid dresses was they needed to be in Louisiana University purple with gold accessories.

Gelly purchased a short dress with a lacy turtleneck and sleeves that perfectly covered up her scars. "I'm not ashamed of them. I just don't want them to take the focus away from you."

"And that is why you are my matron of honor." I kissed her on the cheek. "You look beautiful."

Renee came out then in her chiffon off the shoulder wrap that made use of her height and hugged her curves perfectly. "You look amazing!" Gelly told her. "Marlene won't even be able to tell you're a size or two bigger than me in that dress."

"Kill me now! She did not compare your sizes." Aimee rubbed her forehead in circles.

"Oh, yes, she did. She basically called your bride fat. Luckily, I'm very happy with my size," I said.

"Me too!" Renee added, twirling in her chiffon confection, a Valkyrie on a purple cloud.

Aurelie's dress was a flowy Gunne Sax type dress that gave her a Marie Engles' *Little House on the Prairie* vibe. I thought it a bit too flowy, but since she was twirling around the store grinning from ear to ear, I kept my mouth shut.

The next half hour involved choosing dresses for my sisters, texting said dresses to select, and ordering shoes for all of us. We scheduled a fitting for us next week and another for my sisters the day before the wedding. And as the pièce de résistance, we selected off the rack pieces for the Littles, two adorable dresses for our flower girls and a very debonair suit for Tanner.

Once we got back to the farm, the fun continued because we got Valerie and Bailey Marie to try on their dresses. They looked adorable. Tanner, however, was not amenable to giving us a fashion show.

He stomped his foot. "Why do I have to wear a stupid suit?"

Etienne grabbed him up in a fireman's hold and brought him over to Beau's house. Tanner and all the men came back later dressed to the nines in their service dress uniforms and Tanner in his adorable suit. We made cat calls as the men escorted Valerie, Bailey Marie and Tanner up and down the porch, aka the catwalk. Overall, a productive and enjoyable day. *I'm getting better at having fun.*

26

The Rehearsal

Beau

We invited too many guests. The Littles, my Krewe, and I set up endless rows of chairs for the ceremony tomorrow. My dad and I made a beautiful bower and after the ceremony, I would move it to my yard to set up an outdoor reading nook for Shell and Valerie. Both of them always carried a book. Having never met Val Hebert, I didn't know much about her, but she raised some amazing kids. Also, Valerie seemed to have learned a lot from Shell; they were two peas in a pod.

"Hey, M. Beau, why did you stop?" Tanner asked.

Setting up another chair, I said, "I was thinking."

Tanner worked to tie the cushion to the seat. "About what?"

Looking down at Tanner, I asked, "What do you think you'll be like when you get older?"

"Well, I will be strong like M. Etienne." He flexed his non-existent biceps.

"Hey, I'm strong too!" I frowned as I placed another chair.

Tanner tied another cushion. "Yes, but M. Etienne is the strongest. He told me so when I asked."

Etienne snorted a few rows over and I rolled my eyes. "M. Etienne and I will discuss that at a later date. For today, I think I would get in trouble if I showed him who was the strongest."

Valerie dropped her cushion and put her hands on her hips and channeled every the teachers in my life. "No fighting!" *Michelle's Mini-me.* I grinned on the inside.

"Understood," I told her, but bumped hard into Etienne as I passed him, since he was snickering too loudly. A troupe of ladies carrying boxes and other strange implements mounted the porch steps to the main house.

Valerie made a squeaky noise, grabbed Bailey Marie's arm and announced, "We gotta go!" And they moved to join the troupe.

"What's going on at the main house?" Etienne asked before I could.

"Beauty!" Bailey Marie called back.

"Impossible," I told her. "You two are already too beautiful." Bailey Marie giggled and Valerie, her usual serious self, ran back and gave me a hug.

"You promise you'll keep us?" she whispered.

"Paperwork has already been approved, your rooms are ready, and most importantly, you three are already in my heart. You aren't going anywhere."

She nodded, closed her eyes and smiled as she hugged me tighter. Then she and Bailey Marie skipped to the house.

"Tanner, you have done enough. Why don't you go into your new room and get acclimated?" I asked him.

"Acclimated?" Tanner grimaced.

"Yes, find out where you like to read..."

Tanner scrunched his nose. "Don't like to read."

"Not even my old comic books? The ones that I had copies of?" Etienne asked him.

"Nerd," Marc whispered.

"Comic books?" Tanner perked up at that.

"Go and look. If you don't like them, I'll take them back," Etienne teased.

"Explore your room. Discover your favorite spot for reading, the perfect corner for playing video games, and don't forget to check out the assortment of Lego and erector sets I got you!" I said.

"Boy's toys!" Tanner ran toward the house.

I chuckled. "Sorry, Mr. Chauvinist, I got Bailey Marie and Valerie the same sets. Doctor's orders."

"Madame Michelle." Tanner took a big long-suffering sigh and headed inside my house … soon to be our house.

"He is going to be a handful," Marc said. He would know. Sofia was a terror. Adorable but *canaille canaille.* [very sneaky]

"Yeah, I'm looking forward to it. Plus, I have my secret weapon. I swear my wife-to-be can get kids to do anything. The world should be happy that she only uses her power for good." We went back to setting up chairs and moving tables.

"Kinda makes me wish I had one of my own to help with Sofia. She is a handful herself. The other day she decided she wanted to put on makeup and, unbeknownst to my mother, she ferreted out a box of permanent markers." Armand, Etienne, and I started laughing.

"Pictures please!" I demanded as the others gathered to see. Marc flipped to one in his phone and we howled. "I couldn't take her out in public. It took over a week before that came off."

"Did she choose black for her lips or is that just the only color she had?" Armand asked.

"Abbey Sciutto."

"Isn't she too young for NCIS?" I asked.

"I thought she was asleep before I would turn it on. Apparently, she was watching from the hall and now she is goth." I was wiping away tears, I was laughing so hard and Armand and Etienne were literally rolling on the ground laughing. "Stop it. It's not funny!"

"Oh, but it is. I adore that little troll," I said.

"Which is why you're her parrain," [godfather] Marc acknowledged.

"Speaking of which, who are the Littles' godparents?" Armand asked. "I would make an amazing parrain!"

With a nod, I told him, "You would, but I don't know. That's an excellent question. I'll ask Shell if she knows."

"Before you do that—" Etienne interrupted, "—I have an update. I didn't want to say anything until all the Littles were gone." We headed to my ... our porch steps.

"Go on, did you find that bastard, Ray?" Marc asked as he sat on his customary step.

Etienne shook his head. "Ray, no but, we have had reports. He seems to be on the run and trying to head out of state. Possibly to the Mexican border."

"So, what is the news?" I asked.

"Doug wasn't even the heir."

"Doesn't surprise me." I shrugged my shoulders. "Shell mentioned he had nieces and nephews that he loved. She thought he was going to leave his fortune to them."

"Not just the nieces and nephews. Did you know Michelle went to read to him in French all the time?" Etienne asked.

"Ms. Ellie Mae told me that. She still goes to the nursing home every Sunday after church to read in French. She started taking Valerie with her and they have coffee afterwards, well, coffee and hot chocolate." I smiled at the image.

Grinning, Etienne went on. "You will be interested to know that he willed the land the school is currently leasing to the school. They no longer need to pay the lease."

I nodded. "Put that in an envelope from Pawpaw Blake on the gift table. If we tell her before the wedding, there will be tears."

Etienne smiled. "Sure enough."

Armand shoved me. "Now, go find out about our soon to be godchildren. I got me some parrain [godfather] plans!"

I walked over to my parents', up the porch steps and into the foyer. I followed the noises towards what my mom called the *parlor*, which was where she allowed unknown guests into her house. The hum of hair dryers and female chatter drifted through the transom window. Upon entering the room, I felt I was in a female lair. Women were getting their hair cut, dried, and styled. Makeup was being applied, taken off and then reapplied. And then there was a, I guess you would call it, spa section. A lady was wrapped in a bathrobe, lounging in a recliner with gunk on her face and cucumber slices on her eyes. Gelly laid next to the recliner on a table getting a massage.

"Testosterone alert!" my mom called out.

I snorted. "Really! That's what I'm reduced to?"

"What's tester rone?" Valerie murmured.

"It means a man has entered the space," Gelly whispered back.

"Umm, is Shell here?" I searched, but she was nowhere to be seen.

The bathrobe-clad lady, with cucumbers on her face, raised her hand while the other ladies pointed to her. "Over here!"

I walked over, not sure how to kiss her. I grabbed her hand and kissed that. Then rolled my eyes at the 'Awws.' "Can I speak with you for a moment?"

"Yes, but I'm not getting up from this chair until it is time for my massage." She pointed to the massage table, which made me look over at Gelly. I glimpsed some side boob and grimaced.

"Agh Gelly, side boob, cover up before I'm scarred for life." At the quick intake of breath from the ladies, I grimaced again.

Gelly just laughed, "I know what that feels like."

I closed my eyes. "I'm an idiot. Sorry Gelly!"

"It's okay, I'm good, Beau. It is just an expression. I'm not made of glass. In fact, I think I'm rather tough."

I kissed her cheek. "Tough as nails, Gelly. I love you."

"Awww," everyone said, and my discomfort level shot through the roof.

Shell read my mind and changed the subject. "Have you met my sisters, Beau? They came in so late and we started so early."

"No, not yet."

She called her sisters over. "This is Nicole, the one with a daughter named after me," she gestured to a tall, lean woman with straight blond hair, literally her opposite. "She is the oldest and lives in Paris in an adorable apartment in the Marais and works in fashion. She has a blog. I'll let you read it one day. Terri," she indicated the one with purple hair, "is the literary one. She is just ten months older than me. She works for a publishing house as an editor in New York." *New Yorker*, I thought. "And Natasha, or Tasha, the baby," Shell beamed at her, "is a brainiac. She is working on her doctorate degree in Applied Mathematics at Louisiana University." Tasha, like Shell, had dark curls cropped a bit shorter than her sister and big eyeglasses, no doubt due to all that studying.

"Impressive," I said as I squeezed Shell's hand and then shook her sisters' hands. Then turned back to Shell. "Can we talk?"

"What's up?" She adjusted her chair, so she was sitting upright.

"Do you know if the Littles have godparents?"

"I hadn't thought of that. I'm not sure. Valerie, sweetie, do you have a minute?"

Valerie ran over. "Oui madame." [yes ma'am]

Shell brushed her bangs out of her eyes. "Did y'all and your mama go to a specific church?"

Valerie shook her head. "No."

"Do you know if your grandparents went to a church?"

Another shake of her head. "I never met our grandparents. Mama told me they were dead."

"So, none of you have *parrains* or nannies [Louisiana for godfather and godmother]?"

"No."

I put my hand on her shoulder. "So Marc, Etienne, and Armand hope to be your parrains, if you would like."

"Yes, please," Valerie said, and she leaned into me and gave me a big hug. Bailey Marie also made her way over to join in. I was getting very used to the Littles' hugs.

Another collective, 'Awww...' set my teeth on edge.

"Ok, on that note, we will talk more about it later. One last question. Shouldn't you be doing this tomorrow, the makeup and such?"

"This is the bachelorette party. It is spa day and we are trying out cuts, hairstyles, and makeup that we want for tomorrow. The Beauty Squad will return tomorrow for the main event."

I gave Shell a kiss and got her greasy mask on my face. "Did not mean to intrude on your party."

"Out with you!" my mom said as she wiped off the mask residue and escorted me out the door.

As I walked across the lawn, I called to my crew, "*Call of Duty* to see who gets to be parrain to which Little and for best man duties!"

"Winner or loser!" Marc called back.

"Winners to be parrain and loser gets to be best man, of course," Armand laughed. "You have to make a speech as best man."

"Double elimination tournament," I said.

$$
27
$$

The Wedding

Michelle

The rehearsal went off without a hitch, leaving me in high spirits. Gelly's revelation about Alex's squeezing her hand that morning made the day even brighter. To unwind and take it easy, I made my way to Beau's house afterwards, to relax and cuddle on his porch. With my parents spending the night to prepare for the wedding, we were limited to kissing, hand holding, and drinking libations. My daddy had given Beau 'the look', so he wouldn't even invite me in ... the coward. However, we still managed to make out on his, soon-to-be-our, porch swing.

When we finally came up for air, I couldn't help but smile. "Magic eight ball says, 'outlook good'."

"Yep."

"Just yep?" Arching a brow, I moved back a bit. You gotta start how you mean to go on.

"Ah ... Just agreeing with you," he panicked.

With a snort, I leaned in for another kiss. "We will work on your wife-talking skills."

"I'll ask your dad to train me."

At that, I hugged him, nibbled his earlobe, and smiled. "You do that. See you tomorrow. I'll be the one in the big white dress." I walked away, but couldn't resist turning halfway to the main house and to steal a glance back at my man. He was sipping his scotch as he watched me. With a saucy smile, I skipped the rest of the way across the lawn to his parents' house.

"They're all asleep. Come back!" he called.

"Tomorrow," I said, and turned to blow him a kiss. Humming, I zipped into the house, my body thrumming. That was close.

The morning of the ceremony Babineaux farm was in chaos. The musicians, all relatives, were warming up and drinking coffee and eating scotch eggs from Black Cafe. That was how we bribed them to get their services for free. They also could choose any leftovers to take home after the ceremony. One thing the Babineaux and LeBlanc families did not skimp on was musical or cooking talent.

With my bridesmaids, I lined up at the back of the church. Across from us were Etienne, Armand, and Renee's brothers, Jeb, Eric, and Kevin. The Babineaux were a prolific family.

"So, how did you get to be the best man?" Gelly asked Etienne.

"I lost to all of them in *Call of Duty*." Etienne told her. Gelly snorted and Etienne smiled.

"Children!" my mama clapped her hands. "Focus, the music is about to start. Let's line you up in pairs." Gelly lined up next to Etienne. We had put them together, hoping to heal the rift between them.

"I'm glad that Alex squeezed your hand, Gelly," Etienne told her.

"Thanks, and I'm sorry I blamed you, rather than those bastards Doug and Ray."

"Gelly, if hating me helped you get through hard times, then hate away. Just know that I will always be there for you." Gelly kissed his cheek. Then my mama was there to wipe off the lipstick, and the music started. I had chosen the Bluerunners' music to walk to *Butterbean* for the brides' maids and *Viens avec moi* [Come with me] for the bridal procession.

My memory was blurry after that. I remembered seeing Beau at the end of the aisle in his dress blues and me trying to hurry toward him when my dad pulled me back. "With the music, Shell, or you will get me in trouble with my wife." I smiled up at my daddy and gave him a kiss on the cheek as I waltzed with him down the aisle. Then I remembered thinking how handsome Beau and his Krewe looked in their service dress. What I vividly remembered, besides kissing Beau, were his vows. I thought we were going with traditional vows, but after I repeated my vows, he pulled out a little white paper and changed the script.

"Shell, *ma chère,* [my dear] I promise to let you always select the music when we drive. If that doesn't prove my love, then let me also say I want your worst. Give me your bad hair days, your burned coffee, your lost keys, your broken copier, your annoyance at the department of education," that got a hoot from the teachers in the crowd, "your lost coats, and whatever malady the little beasties give you. Give me whatever they throw at you, and I will give you my love to make it right. I take you as my wife and the Littles as my children, and I promise to do the best I can and to love you with all my heart." I kissed him then.

"Not yet!" Valerie stage whispered, and we both grinned and turned to Father LeBrun.

"By the power vested in me by the Church and the State of Louisiana, I now pronounce you husband and wife. You may now, officially, as a married couple, kiss the bride."

T he reception in a field next to where we held the ceremony included an elevated wooden dance floor. Before the band started, recordings were used for the first two dances, while the musicians grabbed food from the buffet. For our first dance, we swayed to a mashup of *Mon Aimable Brune* by Bonsoir Catin, a romantic French melody, and *Only You* by Yaz, our special song.

Beau nuzzled my neck. "So how is married life treating you thus far?"

"Not bad. You haven't stepped on my feet."

"Hey, I can dance." And he spun me around.

"That you can," I said, and laid my head on his chest as Bonsoir Catin played about *Vivre le vin, l'amour et les filles.* [Long live wine, love, and girls]

The next dance was with my daddy, with one of his favorite songs, *La valse j'aime* [The waltz I like] by Cleoma Falcon. Daddy admitted, "I like him. I still don't trust him with my baby, but he might grow on me."

"He's a good man, Daddy."

"So everyone keeps telling me, but then there was that night at your garage apartment."

"So you're telling me you and Mama waited until after your wedding to do anything? Doesn't your wedding anniversary always correspond with Nicole's age? But her birthday is seven months after your anniversary. I can do math, Daddy."

"She was a preemie!"

I snickered. "I've seen her birth certificate. She was nearly ten pounds at birth."

"I know, and I'm convinced she just did that to spite us." I leaned my head against his shoulder and shook with laughter.

Daddy let go of my hand so I could dry my eyes. I snickered. "If anyone can put a wrench in plans, it will be Nicole."

As the dance ended, Daddy pinned a $100 bill on my dress. "That's too much, Daddy."

"Knowing you, you will probably spend it on school supplies. Plus, I have to show up your uncles. What you want is a competition to see who pins the most money. And here comes my penny pinching brothers now."

After about an hour of dancing, Beau and I stepped away to eat Jambalaya and corn maque choux and watch everyone else dance. After a few more dances, Etienne rang on his champagne glass to get everyone's attention.

"As you know, I am Beau's best friend. Well, one of them. The other two are apparently better at *Call of Duty* than I am. Hence, I get to give the best man toast." Everyone laughed and someone from the Krewe called out, "Loser!"

Etienne continued, "We can all agree that Beau got the better deal. It's no mystery. Dr. Michelle LeBlanc, Shell, is a catch. And I, having never been married or been in any serious relationships, was hard pressed to find something helpful to say. So I did what any of you would do in that situation. I googled 'wedding toasts'. Thanks to technology, I came across a collection of Jane Austen quotes. Since, I know Shell loves her work. I thought she would appreciate this mash up. So, here it is." He cleared his voice.

"It is a truth universally acknowledged, that a single man in possession of a good fortune must be in want of a wife." Everyone chuckled and Etienne continued. *"My dearest friends, Michelle and Beau, have no notion of loving people by halves. To love is to burn, to be on fire. They found themselves by insensible degrees, sincerely fond of each other, and their happiest hours of their lives were what they spent together. Her heart did whisper that he had done it for her. That perhaps it was their imperfections that make them so perfect for one another. Let me assure you, Shell, that Beau*

was one of those who, having once begun, would be always in love. He will make you happy, Shell; I know he will make you happy; but you will make him everything."

More laughter and hoots of agreement sounded as everyone raised their glasses and toasted.

After Etienne, Gelly took the microphone and kissed him on the cheek.

"Wise word, wise words Etienne. Beau, Shell, I'm not much of a speaker. Some people like to talk ... a lot," she pointed to Etienne, "and some people dance."

At that point, all the bridesmaids jumped up and struck a pose on the dance floor. Neil Diamond's *Sweet Caroline* came on and the bridesmaids started to dance a line dance. In front of them, Gelly danced an amazing dance of pirouettes, jetés, and a sprinkle of modern dance elements that synched and mimicked the line dance moves. By the second verse, she asked everyone to join.

"She looks so joyful," he whispered. I looked over at Beau. His sister's joy, which had disappeared after the fire, was the best wedding gift we could have received. He squeezed the bridge of his nose and swallowed hard. I just put my head against his shoulder and watched. I noticed Etienne watching from the corner as he sipped his scotch.

After the bridesmaid's performance, I danced until there was no more room to pin money on my dress. Suddenly, Beau cut in on my great uncle, Nonc Jule, and slowly danced me off the dance floor to the darkened shade of a live oak.

"Run!" he whispered.

As we made a break for his house, Valerie yelled. "They're getting away!" to raucous laughter.

Upon entering the house, we locked the doors, turned off the lights, and raced to the bedroom. While Beau easily stripped out of his clothes, I needed help to unbutton the wedding dress. I had purchased a pink garter belt and corset lingerie set for under my dress. Once Beau unbuttoned and unzipped me, the dress slid off, leaving me in that pink lingerie set.

"I'm gonna need a moment here." He did that spinning motion with his fingers, and I turned to give him a view from all angles. Finding the garter and corset in XL had taken some doing, but based on the look on his face. *Worth it!* He swallowed. "To start, how about we just take off the panties? Then we can strip off other elements, slowly, in the subsequent rounds."

The side of my mouth crooked up. "They have side ties. Just pull."

"You are going to kill me on our wedding night. I already nearly had a heart attack when your lovely dress slipped down and I found you in this pink marvel." He reached hands on either side of my hips and undid the bows holding my undies up. Then he picked me up and threw me on the bed and followed me in.

I loved when he crushed me, his body pinning me down. I wrapped my legs around him to pull him tighter against me, licked his neck, and bit his earlobe.

"Don't linger," I ordered.

"Ah ah ah, you are not in charge. Not tonight anyway."

"Says who?" He grabbed both my wrists with one hand and caressed his way down my body with the other. When he got to my core, he entered me with two fingers. I was wet.

"This says," he explained, licking his fingers and then leaning down for a deep kiss. I could taste myself on his tongue. He kept fingering me as he kissed my lips, my ears, my neck, and my breasts.

"I think I need use of both my hands." He moved each of my hands to grab hold of an iron bar on his headboard. "Don't move your hands or I will have to tie them," he said and then kissed his way down my body. Using one hand for support, he licked into me while the fingers explored inside me for sensitive areas. He discovered one. From there, it took very little for an orgasm to rupture through me. He kissed his way back up my belly, nuzzled my breasts, and kissed me. Then he positioned my limp body how he liked it, spreading my arms and legs akimbo.

"That's how I like you, Shell. All floaty and open." He pushed into me then, as he reached between us to pull out another orgasm from the aftershocks and following up with his own.

"I got you, Shell," he whispered as we both recovered. "I'll always have you." And he kissed me hard, deepening the kiss.

"Always," I smiled, and then demanded, "Again!"

28

Epilogue &
Au suivant
[The next one]

Michelle

Beau, the Littles, and I were in sync and ridiculously happy. Still, I needed some chill girl time, so every morning the porch was my domain where I drank coffee with my girlfriends. With my coffee in hand, my friends and I chatted, taking in the breathtaking sunrise as we prepared ourselves for the chaos of another day. Gelly was always there, but sometimes, Aurelie and Renee stopped by. The Littles called her Tante Gelly, except Val, who called her Nanny [Godmother], and they always seemed to lift her spirits. After school, I also escaped to the porch during the Littles 'tranquility time'. Gelly and I were on the porch tonight. Almost every night, she would stop by to talk or give us an update on Alex. Swishing through the porch door with two steaming mugs, I handed her one. "Here you go. Here is an Irish, Italian hot chocolate."

"Irish and Italian?" Gelly smiled.

"Yes, with Bailey's and Amaretto liqueur." It smelled divine, like dark, rich chocolate. I longed to taste it.

She took a sniff, smiled, and then she took a sip. She hummed as she savored the flavor. "Yummy! Thank you." She peered over at my cup. "Yours looks different."

My grimace said it all. "Mine is herbal tea."

"Yuck, why just why?" Gelly stilled and then lifted her eyebrow and I gave her a crooked smile. "No! You've only been married a few months. When are you due?"

Grinning, I put my hated tea down and held up six fingers. "In six months."

"Oh congratulations. I'm so happy for you and for me. Being an aunt is the best! Wait an eight-month gestation?"

"Yes," I deadpanned. "It's a miracle-baby. Scoot over." We chuckled as we sat and rocked on the porch swing together. Looking out at the night sky and listening to the breeze blow through the leaves and the crickets chirp, I laid my head on Gelly's shoulder.

I nibbled on my bottom lip. "Can I ask you a question, Gelly?"

"Shoot," she said, taking a pull from her spiked hot chocolate.

"Beau and I were talking, and we wanted to know ... if it's a boy ... could we call him Alex?" Her eyes filled with tears and her lip trembled. "No, no, don't cry. I promised Beau I would not make you cry. You know he hates to see you in pain."

"Tough for him. I cry. He needs to deal. But to answer your question, Alex will be so psyched! I'll tell him tomorrow." She hugged me tightly.

"So, good tears?"

She nodded against my head. "Good tears." Then I started crying as well. *Stupid pregnancy hormones.* At that moment, the patio door swung open. Beau walked out, looked at us both in tears, and walked back into the house. He called over his shoulder.

"Told you it would make her sad."

"I'm not sad, *couillon,* [idiot] I'm overwhelmed!" Gelly yelled back at him and I giggled.

Gelly and I settled back down on the porch swing together, and I grabbed her hand. "You know, if you want to get away. You could go to Sainte Anne this summer and learn French. Sea air, cooler temps, and they have afternoon dance classes as part of the language workshops. You should consider it."

"I can't be away from Alex. Maybe later after … I mean, after the baby arrives?"

I nodded. "Absolutely. We'll see how it goes."

"You won't need help?" she asked.

"Please! Between the mothers and your cousins, I'll barely get a chance to hold the baby. Not to mention Beau's Krewe. Since they have become the parrains of the Littles, they're always underfoot."

She chuckled and then sighed. "Then I think I might go. If I need a change of scenery." We hung out on the porch for the rest of the night. Well, until started to fall asleep on Gelly's shoulder and she called Beau to come and put his sleepy, pregnant wife to bed.

Sneak peek: If you just want to bask in that happy HEA feeling, stop here! Otherwise, read the beginning of Angelle's transformation.

Angelle

While my wounds have healed, all I'm left with are the scars. Alex never recovered. He woke up, but he had severe brain damage. The doctors put him in hospice care and I visited every day. He would squeeze my hand and lay his head against my shoulder every day. I took a leave of absence from work to stay near Alex, but I don't know if I'll be going back.

My physical therapist was pushing me to use my dance background to physically recover and something about the dancing also helped my soul heal. While Alex was in hospice, I would show him my new dance moves and run through the numbers I was learning. His eyes were open, so I'm choosing to believe he saw them.

October was line dancing, November was Latin dancing, December was polka.

In December, I rushed to the hospital to show Alex my new polka dance move. Alex loved polka. While I was always skeptical, I smiled. I showed him my moves and then went to sit beside. He put his head on my shoulder and sighed. He breathed his last breath and died with his head on my shoulder six months after the attack. Every day, I thank God for the time I had to say goodbye.

I'm thinking that I'm going to be in pain for a while. Part of me wanted to feel guilt. Alex was an accountant, for God's sake, not a social worker. My job endangered him, but I was talking with Etienne the other night, hanging on Beau and Shell's porch, and he told me,

"If I had a wife, I would have wanted to go like Alex. Giving up my life to gain a few precious seconds to save hers." Since Alex was his cousin, I figured he would know, so I'm letting go of the guilt.

That night after he died, I walked home to my cleared living room and poured out my grief and happiness onto the tiny dance floor. As I danced, I couldn't breathe, but I continued. Tears were streaming down my face and I continued, and then the music changed. I took a deep breath and remembered my life with Alex.

My mind played a movie of when I met him, how he romanced me with hayrides and zydeco dance halls. Finally, I relived how he listened to me, and squeezed my hand while in hospice. I felt him then ... felt his featherlight kisses on my earlobe and his hands ruffle my red curls.

My hair had grown out now. To cover my scars, but also because I was a new person. Dance over, I resolved to start my life anew. That night I registered for Ste. Anne's French Immersion program and I resigned from my job. I looked across the lawn to my brother's family's house. I might never have what Beau has, but I can rebuild my life.

For the rest of Angelle's story, check out "Dance of Love" using the QR code on the next page.

Also by Gigi Hodge

Louisiana L'Amour Series

Learning to Love: Book 1
Dance of Love: Book 2
Thrown into Love: Book 3
Noël in Love: Book 4
Storm of Love (Novella)
Louisiana L'Amour Omnibus

Louisiana Small Town Romance

The Magic of Chemistry

The Babineaux Brothers

Bayou Catfish

About the Author

Growing up in French Louisiana, Gigi was always a reader. But writing also played a role in her life once she began teaching. She worked with the National Writing project as a teacher and then helped to run a program as a professor. She participated in several Nanowrimo experiences (write a novel in a month) throughout the years. However, after she retired in November 2022, she finally listened to her inner voice and challenged herself to become a published writer.

Important to note: Since Gigi now lives abroad, she often uses her writing to connect to her home and experiences in Louisiana. Most of the restaurants and food in her work are not fictional places, although some of them have closed. Go eat there! You will appreciate the Louisiana cuisine. Coming from a French Louisiana background, Gigi also includes the occasional French word or expression. She plans to create a Louisiana French bookmark to highlight her most used Cajun/Creole vocabulary.

Thanks

No author is an island. It takes a team to pull together a book. I want to thank mine. So, thanks to my Beta Readers, Rebecca Klug, Adela, and Nicole whose insights have been invaluable. I also want to thank the All Write Well team for their support and instruction to help me learn how to move from being a hobby writer into a published author.

www.ingramcontent.com/pod-product-compliance
Lightning Source LLC
Chambersburg PA
CBHW020023310726

48970CB00007B/2181